D1188049

PHILIP REEVE
UTTERLY DARK
DARK
AND THE
HEART OF THE WILD

David Fickling Books

31 Beaumont Street
Oxford OX1 2NP, UK

UTTERLY DARK AND THE HEART OF THE WILD
is a
DAVID FICKLING BOOK

First published in Great Britain in 2022 by
David Fickling Books,
31 Beaumont Street,
Oxford, OX1 2NP

www.davidficklingbooks.com

Text © Philip Reeve, 2022

Cover and inside art by Paddy Donnelly

978-1-78845-286-1

1 3 5 7 9 10 8 6 4 2

The right of Philip Reeve to be identified as the author of this work has been
asserted in accordance with the Copyright, Designs and Patents Act 1988.

Papers used by David Fickling Books are from well-
managed forests and other responsible sources.

DAVID FICKLING BOOKS Reg. No. 8340307

A CIP catalogue record for this book is available from the British Library.

Typeset in 12/16pt Goudy by Falcon Oast Graphic Art Ltd
Printed and bound in Great Britain by Clays Ltd, Elcograf S.p.A

To Liz Cross, for guiding this and so many of my
other stories through the wild woods.

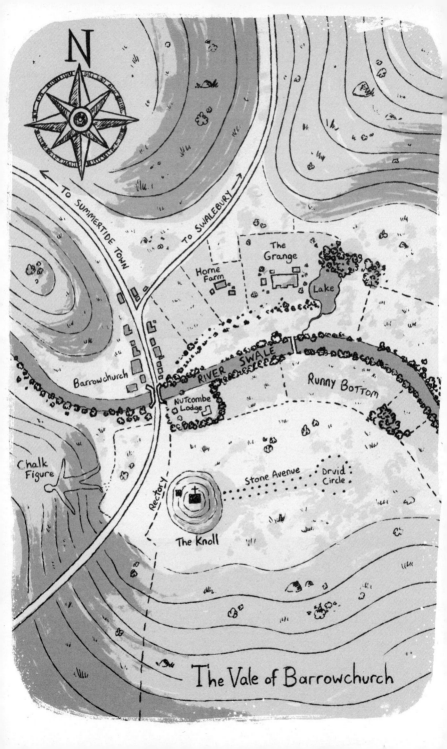

1

THE STORM ON SUMMERTIDE

Dusk was settling upon the downs as Figgy Dan came to the crest of the giant's hill. Below him in the twilight, a tree-lined river snaked its way through the broad valley. On the far side of the river lay a village, and a big house with a lake in its grounds. Figgy had passed that way before. The village was called Barrowchurch, and the people at the big house had been kind to him; they had given him a hot meal and a hot bath. So he tugged his pink coat tighter to keep out the wind and started down the track, past the huge chalk figure that the people of olden times had carved into the hillside there.

The pink coat was a very shabby coat, but then Figgy Dan was a very shabby man. His hair was long and tangled, and his face was hidden by a straggling beard. Tin cooking pots dangled and jangled from the old sheepskin pack he carried. He walked in an odd, jerky way, and he stopped sometimes to strike his own head, or box his ears. 'Oh, leave me be, won't you!' he shouted, although he was entirely alone up there on the downs. 'Oh, won't you never stop your banging and your booming, you old bullroarers?'

The pink coat had been red once, and Figgy had marched in it all up and down the Low Countries, fighting the French. Somehow, during all those battles, the noise of the guns had got inside his head, and when he went home to England it had stayed with him, booming and roaring inside his skull. He could not hear, he could not sleep, he could not hardly think. Trying to escape the din, he fled ever westward, to places more and more remote, until he fetched up at last on Summertide, among the Autumn Isles, a scattering of islands so remote they had been left off the maps entirely, and few people had ever heard of them at all.

The guns in Figgy's head still roared on Summertide, but the noise was fainter here, as if distance from the mainland muffled it a little. Or so it had seemed to Figgy, until this particular October night. Now the booming was louder than ever. 'Shut your noise!' he shouted, as he stumbled down the old chalk road to Barrowchurch, and he started to weep at the thought that all his travels had been in vain and he never would escape his private artillery.

Then he noticed how the wind was gusting over the brow of the down behind him, and how the fading light had taken on a brownish tinge. Glancing back, he saw bruised clouds sprawling across the western sky. A sudden blink of lightning lit the whole world white.

The thunder boomed, and Figgy began to run. He was glad the booming was outside his head this time, but the booming on the inside had left him with a terror of loud noises. Besides, when a man has only one set of clothes, he does not want to be caught out in a storm, and this storm looked set to be a tartar, rushing over the downs on a wind that seemed to have blown up out of nowhere. Figgy had heard strange stories of the haunted seas that lay west of the Autumn Isles. That was where this hurricane had been brewed; he would have wagered money on it, if he'd had any.

By the time he reached the hill's foot and started out across Barrowchurch Common, the thunder was roaring like whole batteries of guns. Hail came down like grape-shot, stinging Figgy's face and ears and hands, striking the road and bouncing high so it could fall down on him again. He would be soaked through or frozen long before he reached the big house.

Then, in a long flash of lightning, he saw the church ahead of him.

Figgy remembered this church from his first visit. It was a spooky sort of church, built on top of a wooded mound that rose out of the broad flatness of the common, unnatural-like. The church seemed to think it unnatural too, for it crouched on the mound's top with the air of a man who'd climbed on the back of a sleeping elephant for a joke and now feared it might wake and throw him off. But it was closer than the village, so Figgy ran towards it.

This being October, the trees had mostly lost their leaves, so the rain pelted him as hard while he climbed the steep side of the mound as it had out in the open. Just as he neared the top and saw the lych gate into the church-yard ahead of him, a bright flash of lightning showed him a lady standing on the path not three yards away.

'Lor' bless us!' said Figgy, and stopped short.

He thought he had seen a ghost. The wooded mound seemed just the place for wandering spirits, and this was just the sort of night they would be wandering on. Besides, it was easier to believe in ghosts than that a fine lady would be out here all alone in such a blow.

But the lightning came again, and reassured him that the lady was not a ghost. Not only that; she was a lady Figgy knew. She was Miss Inshaw, from the big house, where they had been so kind to him. The butler had told Figgy to sling his hook, but Miss Inshaw had come out and said no. Her late father would not have wanted her

4

to turn away any man who had worn the king's uniform, she'd said, and she had sent Figgy round to the stables, where the hot meal and hot bath had happened.

Standing there in the downpour, he felt a little less cold and hungry for just remembering it.

The lightning flashed. At the same instant there came a clap of thunder so loud and so close overhead it made poor Figgy cry out in terror. Miss Inshaw, who had been standing there in the wind and rain as if in a dream, turned and saw him. He backed away, ashamed of his dishevelled state, and made a little bow to show he meant no harm. He did not know if Miss Inshaw recognized him, but he was glad she did not seem afraid of him.

'Can you hear it too, sir?' she asked.

'Meaning the thunder, miss?' said Figgy. 'How could I not?'

'No, no – behind the thunder, and in the gaps between. Listen! Can you not hear fairy music?'

What with the thunder outside his head and his own personal cannonade still booming on within, Figgy could barely hear her voice, let alone any bloomin' fairy music. But Miss Inshaw seemed happy about it, so he nodded, just to please her.

'I knew it!' she shouted, over another rending crash of thunder. 'I have always said that Barrowchurch Knoll is a fairy hill. On a night like this, the fairy folk are sure to be abroad!'

'Begging your pardon, miss,' said Figgy. 'Shouldn't you think about getting indoors? If you don't mind me saying, you'll catch your death out here . . .'

Miss Inshaw did not seem to hear him. She was pointing towards the lych gate. A huge, old oak tree stood next to it, ancient and evil-looking, but she was gazing at it like it was a vision of Paradise.

'Look!' she said. 'Oh, look!'

She stepped off the path and started across the gnarled web of roots that covered the slope below the tree. Afraid for her, afraid for himself, afraid of being left alone with the dreadful thunder, Figgy went after her. Light seemed to be coming from beneath the tree. It was not the jaggedy, fleeting light of the storm but long red-gold shafts. They shone out from a place between the tree's roots as if a door had opened there and somewhere inside the hill the sun was setting on a better day.

'Oh, come see!' Miss Inshaw called, as if Figgy were one of her genteel friends and not just a raggedy tinker man. Figgy started to wonder if she was quite right in the head. But he shyly scrimble-scrambled his way across the wet roots to join her. 'Look!' she said.

The sky split open above them.

Side by side, they stood in the light and stared at something wonderful.

2

THE WEDDING

The wedding had been the talk of the island of Wildsea for months, ever since the excitement of last autumn's awful storm had faded. So many people had come to watch the ceremony that the little church behind the dunes at Marazea was packed to bursting, and the congregation spilled out into the churchyard, and stood upon the churchyard wall, straining to catch the words of the marriage service drifting from inside.

But Utterly Dark heard the service very clearly, for the bridegroom was Utterly's guardian, Uncle Will, and the bride was her friend Aish, and so she had been appointed Chief Bridesmaid. Her friend Lucy Dearlove and Lucy's little sister Emily were bridesmaids too, and they all three stood by Aish's side at the altar, with floral

7

crowns perched on their heads, and the rest of their persons clad in new dresses of sprigged muslin, which Uncle Will had ordered all the way from Bristol for the occasion.

Some of the grander islanders, who lived 'over the hill' on Wildsea's sheltered east coast, had been shocked when Uncle Will and Aish announced their engagement. They had declared it a most scandalous, unsuitable and ill-advised match. After all, the Darks of Sundown Watch had been Watchers on Wildsea for countless generations, and were one of the island's most important families, while Aish was just a troll-woman from the Dizzard hills, and did not even seem to have a surname! But most people rightly sensed that Aish was important too, in her own way, and besides, they knew she had rescued Will Dark when he was washed ashore from a shipwreck the previous year. Since Wildsea people believe that what you save from the sea is yours for ever, it seemed only right and proper they should wed. When Reverend Dearlove read the banns on Easter Sunday there had been a friendly cheer from the rougher elements of the congregation, a murmur of satisfaction from everyone else, and Utterly had been able to nudge Lucy and whisper, 'I *told* you they would soon be married,' which had been extremely gratifying.

'Marriage is not to be entered into unadvisedly or lightly; but reverently, discreetly, deliberately, soberly and in the fear of God,' said Reverend Dearlove, trying to sound stern but not really succeeding, because Will and Aish were among his dearest friends and he was delighted to be marrying them.

Uncle Will looked really almost respectable, thought Utterly, in his new plum-coloured coat and his good white breeches and buckled shoes. As for Aish, her large, strong-featured, somewhat hairy face had grown very much prettier since Utterly first met her, but then perhaps all faces did when you grew to like their owners. Today she looked perfectly beautiful, standing in the sun-beam that came in through a high window to light up the altar. Utterly had been slightly afraid she would wear her head-dress of antlers, which would not have been at all the thing for church, but she had left the antlers off, and the wreath of spring flowers, which Utterly had helped to weave, looked lovely on her dark red hair. She wore a dress of cream silk, which was a gift from Will, and very well it suited her, with Utterly, Lucy and little Emily holding up the train. And if she still had rather a lot of strange trollish charms and ornaments hung around her neck, and carried an unusual bouquet of moss and oak-twigs, nobody minded, for she looked so radiantly happy.

Even Egg, who had been far from delighted when Mrs Skraeveling made him put on shoes and comb his hair flat with water, had brightened when he saw her. 'The whole island is blooming and so is Aish,' he said, and nodded his approval. Egg was only eleven, and Aish was no one quite knew *how* old, but Egg regarded himself as her minder all the same.

'If any man can show just cause, why they may not lawfully be joined together, let him now speak, or else hereafter hold his peace,' said Reverend Dearlove.

Silence fell. The congregation held its breath, praying that no one would know of a reason why the wedding should not happen, but also just *half* hoping that someone *might*, because wouldn't that be thrilling?

And for a moment, Utterly thought someone *was* going to speak, for she heard a sound that was a little like a throat being cleared, or perhaps a roll of far-off thunder, or the low growl of an animal. It was the sort of sound you felt as much as heard, trembling in the cool old granite flagstones beneath her slippers, and thrumming through the wood of the pews.

The sound gave Utterly the feeling that Mrs Skraeveling called 'someone walking over your grave', but which Utterly thought was a certain sign of magic in the air. She looked quickly at the scrubbed, expectant faces of the congregation, but no one else seemed to have heard it. Even Aish, who had sharper ears than most, was gazing lovingly at Will, quite unconcerned.

So perhaps I imagined it, thought Utterly. But she didn't think she had.

'I require and charge you both . . .' said Reverend Dearlove, breaking the silence, and the service went on its sonorous way until at last Will and Aish were married, and the vicar was able to say in his own everyday voice, 'You may kiss the bride, Will!'

'Ugh!' whispered Utterly, Lucy and Egg, looking away. They all thought kissing was perfectly disgusting, and felt quite certain they would never go in for that type of thing when *they* were grown-ups.

But although Will and Aish's kiss was warm and loving, it did not go on for too long. Soon they were outside in the sunshine, accepting the congratulations of neighbours and well-wishers. Then Utterly and her friends were able to look forward to the most important part of the day, which was the food. Utterly and Egg had helped Mrs Skraeveling with the preparations for the wedding breakfast that morning and, as Egg kept telling anyone who would listen, it was going to be a feast fit for Nebuchadnezzar himself. (Egg was not entirely sure who Nebuchadnezzar was, but thought he must be someone pretty grand because he had two Zs in his name.)

So everyone went up the long track to Sundown Watch, the bride and groom riding on a flower-bedecked wagon, the children running beside it, the villagers following, and two of Aish's Dizzard friends playing old, old songs on a fiddle and a flute. The track was steep, the climb hot, but at the top long trestle tables had been set up in the gardens of the Watch, with awnings to shade them, and there was cider, and small beer, and lemonade. The next few hours were mostly talk, and laughter and eating.

But you could have too much of talk and laughter, Utterly discovered, and it turned out that even eating palled after a while – or, at least, there came a point when it seemed wise to take a break from it, in case you burst. The fiddler and the piper were playing reels now, and a few couples were already venturing out to join Will and Aish upon the portion of the lawns that had been set aside for dancing. Utterly left them to it and slipped off alone. She went around the house to the seaward side, then followed the steep cliff-path down into Blanchmane's Cove, wondering what the sea made of it all.

The sea was where Utterly had come from. She had been washed ashore in a basket on the 21st of February twelve years before, when she was just a tiny baby. She had grown into a girl with such dark eyes and such straight silk-black hair that it was generally believed on Wildsea that her parents had been a Chinese merchant and his wife whose ship had foundered in the Western Deeps. But lately she had come to doubt that story. For during the great storm of the previous October she had somehow been washed or carried away from Wildsea and had adventures on the Hidden Lands, those islands that appeared mysteriously sometimes out on the western sea. Those were the islands the Watchers of Wildsea were supposed to watch for, for they were the home of the mysterious and powerful Gorm, who haunted Wildsea's oldest legends.

How she had reached the Hidden Lands exactly, and what she had seen and done there, Utterly could not quite recollect. Nor could Uncle Will or the boy called Egg, who had ventured after her to fetch her home. All the memories of their visit to the Hidden Lands had faded like dreams as soon as they set foot on Wildsea again. But Utterly had been left with the oddest feeling ever since, that her parents had not been merchants at all, and that the ancient power that dwelled in the western deeps had some profound connexion with her. The Gorm *cared* for her. How else could she, and Egg, and Uncle Will have been allowed to come safely home, riding a little frail boat over that angry sea which drowned all ships?

The sea did not look angry as Utterly scrambled down the cliff-path to it on the evening of the wedding. It had been unusually quiet ever since the storm, and today it looked as meek as a kitten and as sleepy as a sloth. It had barely enough energy to push its little wavelets up the sand. Tangles of kelp washed limply in its shallows, and it made no effort to weave them into terrifying weed-men, which it had delighted in doing not so long ago. The white-clad lady who was the Gorm's human form did not rise from the gentle swell offshore to smile at Utterly. And when Utterly stood on the wet sand at the water's edge and announced, 'Uncle Will and Aish are married now,' the sea did not answer her, or show the slightest interest.

Utterly missed it. She missed its moods, and its rages. She missed its terrors. Last October it had risen in such a fury that it had torn down the cliff outside her bedroom window and flattened the vicarage, and people had found seaweed hanging from the trees three miles inland. Now it had grown so lazy that the fishermen of Merriport were starting to talk about sailing their boats around Gull Point and fishing in the western deeps. None of them had mustered the courage to actually *do* it yet, but they were *talking* of doing it.

It was as if the Gorm was sulking. Or perhaps she was so lonely out there in her half-imaginary Hidden Lands that she had given way to melancholia, and no longer had the heart to brew up storms and tear tall sea-cliffs down?

Perhaps I should go to her, thought Utterly, feeling suddenly sorry for the lonely and terrible old Gorm. All she need do was wade out into those little waves and set off swimming for the far horizon. The Hidden Lands would be waiting for her there, just out of sight.

For a moment, the temptation was very strong. She even took a step or two towards the sea's edge. But before the gentle waves could touch her slippers, a voice from behind her called, 'Utterly!' and she looked round to see Egg waving frantically from the clifftop.

'Utterly!' he yelled, 'Aish and your uncle are setting off to ride to the Dizzard. And I have saved you a helping of that fruit pudding!'

3

THE BLACK STAG

Aish was not about to spend her wedding night beneath a roof: neither the slate roof of Sundown Watch, nor even the good mossy thatch of her own long-house at Dizzard Tor. Instead, she and Will left their horses at the Trollbridge Inn and went up by secret ways through clefts in the crags and down to the tarn that lay cupped in the Dizzard's heart, hidden from the sea by steep, wooded slopes. Aish kept a tiny boat there, tied up to the tree roots on the lake shore.

'I did not think that you approved of boats,' said Will, when he was settled on its single thwart and the boat was gliding out from the shadows of the trees.

Aish, standing in the stern with the one long oar, looked fondly down at him and said, 'I do not fear good fresh water. I would never set out in any boat across the old Gorm's salty, restless, and revengeful sea. Not that we have heard much of the old Gorm since you defeated her.'

Will laughed, a little nervously. 'I wish I could remember that. You make it sound most heroical.'

'But you *were* heroical that night, Will Dark. Do you really not recollect how the Gorm, in all her rage and enormousness, came wading ashore, and how you and I met on the dunes, and near got trampled by her, and how you struck her down with Egg's little hunting spear?'

'I remember *something*,' said Will, knitting his brow with the effort of it. 'I remember the wind, and the driving spray, and the dune collapsing under me so I was half buried. I remember you digging me out, and being so strong and such a comfort to me. But as to the rest . . .'

'You must remember how the Men o' Weed stole Utterly away, and you went after her in the witch's boat? How you got her back I do not know, since I could not go with you over the cold old sea, but get her back you did. You *must* remember.'

'I remember ruffians attacked Sundown Watch, and the Skraevelings were never able to describe their faces. I remember that Utterly was washed away . . . I remember a grand building somewhere . . . Or was it only a sea cave?'

'It was the Hidden Lands, my love,' said Aish. 'It was the home of the Gorm, and you were so brave for going

17

there. But that place is like the land of dreams; it is hard to bring clear memories home with you.'

There was an island in the tarn's centre, a dome of old trees which seemed to float upon the layer of mist that hung just above the water. The boat's keel grounded on the shingle at its edge. Will scrambled out and turned back to help Aish out, but she was not the sort of lady who required much help, and she was already wading ashore with her wedding dress hitched up to keep it dry. He followed her a little way through the trees, and there in the middle of the island was a deep pool, filled with reflections of the afterglow that was still gilding the edges of the clouds high above. In the middle of the pool was a small island, where white flowers showed among the grass, and there, blankets and rugs had been laid upon the ground and an awning pitched over them to preserve them against the evening dew.

'Is this place a dream too?' asked Will.

'It is a place of power, Will Dark,' said Aish. 'An island on a lake on an island on a lake on an island . . . This is my place, and nothing can trouble us here. Now, do you want to stand all night talking? For it is getting late, and look, the evening star is peeking through the trees at us, and won't she be disappointed in us if all we do upon our wedding night is talk?'

❖

The evening star very bright in the west, the sea perfectly empty, wrote Utterly. She was sitting upon her high stool on the platform that Mr Skraeveling had built beside the ruins of the Watcher's Tower, demolished by last autumn's storm. She had watched the western horizon through Uncle Will's telescope until the sun set, and she had seen nothing except the long light changing on the sea and the first stars coming out. She knew the Hidden Lands were out there, but it seemed they were hidden even more completely than before.

Before the light died altogether she added another note to her entry in the Log. *Mr William Dark, the Watcher on Wildsea, was Married today to Aish of Dizzard Tor.* She drew a heart beside the words to celebrate. After eight months of perfectly empty seas, it felt nice to have an item of interest to enliven the pages of the Watcher's Log.

Aish dreamed that she stood on the shore of her little island, looking out across the water. The mist had gone. The tarn was a mirror, and the trees on its far shore were very still and dark. Even Aish, with her sharp eyes, stood looking for a while before she made out the shape of the big black stag that stood watching her from the water's edge.

'What have you come back for?' Aish spoke firmly, but

if Will or Utterly had heard her they would have recognized the faint tremble of uncertainty in her voice, as if she were afraid. But only the black stag heard. It took a step into the clear water, as if it intended to swim out to the island. Aish had forgotten how big it was, how wide its antlers, like the crown of a dead tree. There were no stags like that left in the world any more, although they had been common once.

'You are out of fashion,' she told it. 'Run home, wherever your home is nowadays.'

The stag dipped its antlers, as if in respect, but really just to show her how very sharp they were, and how very many points they had. Its eyes burned with a golden light that was somehow both cold and fiery at once.

Aish awoke. The awning glowed gently with the light of the new day creeping across the sky above the tarn. The memory of her dream was very real. She rose, careful not to wake Will, and went through the trees to the place where she had stood in her dream. There were no hoofprints on the far shore where the stag had stood; no spreading ripples in the water; no trampled grass or broken branches to mark the place where such a large animal had made its way down to the tarn. So the stag had not been real. But Aish knew that did not mean it had not been *there*.

'You old villain,' she said. 'Wildsea has done well enough without you all these many years. Where were you when the old Gorm came rampaging, eh? We might have used you then. But not now. Stay out of my dreams. Stay out of my woods. Stay in your own world. Leave this one be.'

4

AN INVITATION

There followed honeyed months of golden sunlight, with the bees all a-buzz among the buttercups and bluebells. The newlyweds spent whole weeks up in the Dizzard woods or exploring down the coves and cliffs of the east coast, very much delighted with each other's company. The rest of the time they stayed at Sundown Watch, where Will still had to oversee the repairs to the house and the rebuilding of the Watcher's Tower.

With so much going on, Utterly's schooling somehow got overlooked, which suited Utterly very well. The Dearlove family was still living at the Watch while they waited for their new vicarage to be finished, but Mrs Dearlove's time was taken up with choosing wallpapers and carpets, and her husband had many more weddings to perform, for it was turning out to be a famous year for weddings on Wildsea. Their children, Lucy, Emily and Horatio, were left as free as Utterly. As for Egg, he had never had much time for schooling, and came and went between Sundown Watch and the Dizzard as he pleased, so the five of them were able to run wild together. They built themselves a camp in the spinney on St Chyan's Common. They invented a game called Urgles, which combined elements of cricket, hurling, tag and croquet, and played it for hours in the lengthening evenings on the flat piece of garden where the dancing had been. One day, they traced Stinlake Brook all the way to its soggy beginnings among the bog-cotton and curlew nests on Owlsbarrow Beacon, and planted a flag there in the peat to claim it for King George. Utterly sensed the time was coming when she would be too dignified and grown-up for such pursuits, but it had not come yet, and she was determined to enjoy childhood while it lasted.

And in the end, it was not growing up that put a stop to the games and expeditions. It was a letter, delivered one afternoon by a boy who had ridden over from Merriport.

Letters were something of a rarity at Sundown Watch, especially letters like this one, written on heavy, thick-woven, creamy paper, and sealed with a blob of red wax on which a coat of arms had been impressed. Everyone gathered around Will in the drawing room as he broke the seal.

'It is from my cousin,' he said, after a moment.

'I did not know you had a cousin, Will,' said Reverend Dearlove.

'Yes – although he lives on Summertide, and I have not seen him since I was quite small. His name is Francis Inshaw. He had a sister, Elizabeth, but she died last autumn. I believe Francis is still in mourning, and that is why he could not attend the wedding. He sent us his good wishes, though, and a handsome present – it was Cousin Francis who gave us the silver milk jug, Aish.'

'And why is he writing now?' asked Aish. 'Does he want it back?'

Will studied the letter. 'He says, *My dear Cousin, I give you joy of your marriage* – etcetera, etcetera – ah, here is the meat of it, listen: *I write in the hope that you may be able to assist me with some Druidic monuments which are sited on my land. Our parson, Dr Hyssop, advises me that these relics of the distant past may be of interest to antiquaries and, further, that they may mark sites where our heathen ancestors buried their dead and, indeed, that they may contain gold, jewels and other valuables. I know nothing of these matters, but I collect that you have made a study of such relics, and so I write to suggest that you and the new Mrs Dark might be so kind as to pay me a visit here on Summertide and give me your opinion of our various earthworks . . .'*

'What does all that mean?' asked Egg, who had grown rather lost among all the long words.

'It means Uncle Will and Aish are invited to

Summertide!' said Utterly. (And how exciting that sounded! And how she wished *she* were invited too!)

Will looked happy at the prospect, but only for a little while. When he lived in England he had developed a great enthusiasm for antiquities, and geology, and astronomy, and all the other mysteries that gentlemen of science were learning to unravel in this exciting new nineteenth century. Returning to Wildsea, his enthusiasm had prompted him to make a detailed description of the stone circle that crowned St Chyan's Head. In his eagerness, he had written up his discoveries in a hasty letter and mailed it to the *Island Post* on Lamontane. But by the time it was published, St Chyan's Head had been destroyed, taking the circle with it, and Will had learned that some mysteries were a great deal more mysterious than gentlemen of science imagined.

'My cousin Inshaw must have seen my foolish letter in the *Post*,' he said. 'That is why he thinks me an authority on such matters.'

'So will you go to Summertide and advise him on these stones?' asked Mrs Dearlove. 'I remember you were all afire about antiquities and Druid temples when you first came home to us from London.'

'Until I learned not to meddle in such things,' said Will.

There was a brief, uneasy silence. Everyone was thinking of what had happened the previous autumn. Mrs Dearlove suddenly remembered how the old vicarage had been flattened, not by the wind, but by a vast, angry woman woven out of weed. Utterly was recalling strange glowing figures she had seen in the depths of the sea. Will had a vision of a beautiful palace on an unknown shore. But here in the drawing room, with the summer sun shining in, those memories seemed so hazy, and so unlikely, that they must surely be only the memories of dreams, and everyone felt too shy to speak of them.

Aish chuckled and said, 'Well, I think you should go, Will Dark.'

'You do?'

'I do! There can be no harm left in old graves and mounds on Summertide, for magic does not linger on those soft eastward isles the way it does on Wildsea.'

'And shall you come with me, Aish? We might take a tour of all the islands on our way . . .'

Aish laughed. 'Not I, Will Dark! What, leave my woods, and travel over all that wide restless wobbling waste of sea? You know I cannot. I am of the land, and I always shall be. But I do not want to keep you prisoner here, my love. I have business to attend to in my woods, so go you to Summertide, and come back to me, and I shall welcome you home with a heart grown even fonder for the absence.'

'Well . . .' said Will doubtfully, wanting to make it clear that he would miss her, and would not go unless she was absolutely sure.

'I am sure,' said Aish.

'I will come with you, Uncle Will!' Utterly said eagerly.

'I have never had a holiday before. I have never visited another island . . .' (Her voice trailed away then, because she was thinking of the Hidden Lands, but her memories of them were so foggy that she did not think they had counted as a holiday.) 'You cannot possibly go alone. I will come and keep you company.'

'That is a very good idea,' said Aish.

'The voyage may be uncomfortable,' Will warned. 'Why, the last time I ventured aboard a ship it was wrecked beneath me . . .'

'And it was me who found you all blue and bedraggled on the sand, if you recall,' said Aish. 'But with the sea in its present mood of meekness and mildness there is little danger. And though the old Gorm does not have much power over those eastward seas, she must have some, I reckon, and that is another reason to take Utterly with you. The Gorm has a kindness for Utterly, and if Utterly goes with you I am sure no harm will come to you upon the waves.'

'But . . .' said Uncle Will, and Utterly knew he was thinking up further reasons why they should not go, but she could also tell he really wanted to. She clenched her fists by her sides, and hopped from foot to foot with impatience, until he turned and caught her eye.

'Well, Utterly?' he asked. 'What is your opinion? Do you really wish to make this trip to Summertide?'

'I should like it above all things,' said Utterly, and she nodded very firmly.

5

THE VOYAGE

Preparing for a holiday took almost as much time and bother as preparing for a wedding. First Uncle Will had to write a reply to Mr Inshaw, and hurry it over to Merriport so it could be taken to Summertide aboard the packet ship. Then there were clothes to be washed and pressed, and dusty, musty, cobwebby old trunks and portmanteaux to be unearthed from the depths of the box room and scrubbed until they were fit to be packed. Mrs Skraeveling insisted on altering Utterly's best summer frock, which had grown strangely too short for her since last year. Uncle Will had to give detailed instructions to the builders working on the Tower. Utterly had to tutor Mrs Dearlove, who would be Acting Watcher while she and Uncle Will were gone abroad. (Utterly carefully showed her how to note her observations in the new volume of the Watcher's Log, and felt glad the previous volume was buried somewhere beneath the rubble of the fallen Tower. Some of the observations noted in that had been very strange indeed.)

At last, all was ready. Will and Utterly left Sundown Watch very early on a fine July morning, with Will riding on the Dearloves' horse, and Utterly perched behind Mr Skraeveling on the wagon that was carrying their luggage. Mrs Skraeveling and the Dearloves waved from the gateway, and Lucy, Emily and Horatio ran behind for a while. Aish strode along beside Will, for she was going all the way to Merriport to wave the travellers off. So was Egg, who sat behind Utterly on the wagon, sulking.

'I still do not see why I can't come to Summertide with you,' he said.

'Because Summertide is not like Wildsea, Egg,' Aish told him. 'A grand gentleman like Mr Francis Inshaw will not want barefoot boys scampering around his fine house. He would make you sleep in the servants' quarters. Or in the kennels with his dogs.'

'I don't mind,' said Egg. 'I like dogs.'

'Well, you cannot go,' said Aish, 'and that is that.'

'It is only for a week or two, Egg,' said Utterly. 'Then we will be back.'

Egg grunted, unconsoled, and would not look at her. The road was growing steep, and the Dearlove children wearied of following and stood waving. 'Goodbye! Goodbye!' Utterly turned to wave back, and had her last glimpse of Sundown Watch looking very small behind her, like a toy house balanced on its clifftop with the blue of the western sea behind.

Then the road led over a shoulder of the hills, and the eastern sea came into view ahead, looking just as calm and blue, but speckled all over with islands. When she saw them, just for a moment, Utterly felt her heartbeat quicken. But those were not magical islands, and there was no need to hurry home and write her sightings of them in the Log. They were Wildsea's more civilized neighbours: Finnery, Holt, Gorsedd and Seapitts. And one of those vague ones, very far off in the haze, must be Summertide . . .

The sadness that had come on Utterly when she left her friends and home behind struggled for a moment with the excitement of the journey ahead, and the excitement won. Soon, as the road wound down through Long Wood, she could see the brightly painted houses of Merriport below her, and the harbour where a little ship lay moored.

The ship was named the *Whimbrel*, and her master was named Captain Varley. He was waiting on the quay to welcome his passengers; a black man in a blue coat and an old fashioned, three-cornered hat. A gold tooth flashed when he grinned. He looked exceedingly like a pirate to

Utterly, but at least he seemed a friendly one. His crew lifted the heavy trunks down from the wagon as if they weighed no more than feather pillows, then ran nimbly aboard with them by means of a wobbly little bridge they called a gangplank. Aish hugged Will goodbye, and Utterly was half inclined to hug Egg. But Egg seemed suddenly to have disappeared, probably because he had guessed there would be hugging going on. There was no time to look for him because Captain Varley was eager to catch the tide, which would wait for no man, he said.

So Utterly hugged Aish extra hard, and told her to give Egg her love, and then went up the gangplank after Uncle Will. Sailors bellowed nautical remarks at one another; things were belayed and cast off, sails were hoisted, the gangplank was hauled aboard, and the *Whimbrel* began to move slowly, slowly away from the quay. Utterly shaded her eyes against the sun to watch the sailors scrambling about in the rigging, and by the time she remembered to turn and wave to Aish, Merriport was surprisingly far behind her, and Aish was just a tiny figure right at the end of the harbour wall, with one hand raised above her head in farewell.

There was still no sign of Egg.

'The Gorm is looking kindly on us,' said Captain Varley, rapping his knuckles on the wood of the gunwale for good luck. 'She has sent us a gentle sea, and a fair wind. We shall have you at Summertide afore nightfall.'

Utterly thought how surprised he would be if he knew she had actually met the Gorm, who was just a legend of the sea to him. But had she really met her, or had it been just dreams? She decided not to mention it, and made her way to the front of the ship, enjoying the smells of tar and sea. Doing her best to keep out of the busy sailors' way, she watched the dunes and hills of Hoyt go by, and then the grim grey cliffs of Finnery. A playful dolphin kept pace with the *Whimbrel* for a while, appearing first on one side of the ship and then the other. Once in the distance she saw a steamboat unspooling a white streamer of smoke from its chimney. It was a nasty, dirty, contume-lious contraption, said Captain Varley, and would never catch on.

Around noon they went below to the captain's cabin and ate luncheon at his table, which dangled from the roof on ropes rather than standing on legs like a normal table, and had ingenious batons nailed around its edges to stop the plates from sliding off as it swung to and fro. The batons were not really necessary that day, for the motion of the ship was so gentle that the table barely swung at all, and Utterly had two portions of pie and felt not a trace of seasickness. Captain Varley said she was a natural sailor, which pleased her very much. He also said that Summertide was a fine place: his mother had run a tavern on the harbour there, while his father had been a sailor from who-knew-where – parrots and monkeys had featured in the tales he told of it, whenever his voyagings brought him back to Summertide Town. Captain Varley had followed in his footsteps, sailing all the seven seas before he settled for a simpler life among the Autumn Isles. He had even served aboard a man-o-war and fought in the famous fleet action in Aboukir Bay.

'You were at the Battle of the Nile?' said Uncle Will, much impressed. 'What can you tell us of it?'

'Well, sir, not much, in all honesty, for I was below decks, serving a gun aboard HMS *Bellerophon*. The '*Billy Ruffian*', we foremast hands called her. A gun-deck is a busy place in battle, and all I recall of the day is noise and smoke and heat and hurly-burly . . .'

Here Captain Varley paused, as if searching his memory. Utterly wondered if memories of battles were as hard to hold on to as memories of magic. Then, mingled with the other noises of the ship, she heard a sound from behind her. There was a cupboard there, whose door stood slightly open, and the small noises coming from within suggested that something was alive inside, and trying very hard not to make any small noises.

Captain Varley had found the thread of his story again, but Utterly was more interested in the cupboard now. At first she was afraid it was a rat in there, but it sounded too big – she was almost certain she could hear it breathing. She began to wonder if it could be the ship's cat. Cautiously, for fear of scratches, she reached out and swung the cupboard door open. Crouched inside, watching her with wide eyes and a finger pressed to his lips to shush her, was Egg.

'Why, Egg!' she said, too astonished to pay attention to the finger.

Captain Varley broke off his story, sprang across the cabin with a shout, and dragged the boy out of the cupboard by the collar of his grubby shirt. 'A stowaway!' he roared.

'It weren't me, I ain't done nothin',' squealed Egg. 'Which I just came on board to have a look around, didn't I, and I must have fell asleep is all . . .'

'It is all right, Captain,' said Uncle Will. 'This boy is known to me. Now, Egg, whatever were you playing at?'

Egg looked sullenly at the deck and muttered, 'Didn't want you going off without me, did I? Going off to foreign parts an' all.'

'But, Egg, you know you cannot come with us! Mr Inshaw will be expecting only me and Utterly, not a party of three. Captain Varley, I shall have to ask you to take Egg back to Wildsea with you.'

'Very well,' said Varley, still gripping Egg firmly by the shirt collar. 'You wouldn't rather I keelhaul him then? Or hang him from the yardarm? Or give him sixty lashes with a rope's end?'

'Oh, I don't think that's necessary,' said Uncle Will. 'Egg meant no harm.'

'If you say so,' said the captain. He let go Egg's collar, ruffled his hair, and said, 'You'd best run along to the galley then, you young scoundrel, and see if cook has any of that pie left. And you go with him, miss, to make sure he gets into no more mischief on the way.'

As Utterly led him through the narrow passage to the galley Egg muttered, 'That was a joke, wasn't it? About the hanging and flogging and heel-calling and all that?'

'I *think* it was,' said Utterly. 'You do deserve it, though. Whatever got into you?'

'*Somebody* has to come and keep an eye on you in foreign parts,' said Egg.

'Well it won't be you, Egg. You heard what Uncle Will said. As soon as we dock at Summertide he's going to send you straight home again.'

Egg snorted. 'No he ain't. He's too kind hearted. You'll see.'

Egg was right. By that evening, Will's determination to be stern had softened. He came to find Egg and Utterly in a sort of nest they had made for themselves among some ropes and empty chicken coops near the *Whimbrel*'s bows and said, 'Very well, Egg. You have come this far, so you may as well come all the way. But I shall have to introduce you as my servant, not a fellow guest. And don't imagine a grand house like Mr Inshaw's will be as free and easy as we are at Sundown Watch.'

'Thank you, Will Dark!' said Egg, grinning from ear to ear.

'Well,' said Will, 'it is not the first time you have disobeyed your elders and betters to follow me to sea, is it? And I was glad enough of your company before.' He took out his watch and checked the time. 'Captain Varley tells me we should soon come within sight of Summertide. We shall stay tonight at his family's inn, and tomorrow find a carriage to take us to my cousin's house. It is at a place called Barrowchurch.'

'Land ho!' yelled someone high up in the rigging.

Utterly and Egg turned to look. The dolphin was back, dancing in the bow-wave, and upon the sea ahead, the high white cliffs of Summertide gleamed in the evening sun like a smile of welcome.

6

THE STARS LOOK DOWN

Summertide Town lay in a broad bay with the bone-white cliffs rearing up on either side. A river came down out of the island's heart there, the Swayle, broad and slow, carrying its pale silt far out to sea. The harbour was much bigger than Merriport, and filled with shipping of all sorts; barques from Finnery, a schooner out of Hoyt, even an elderly Royal Navy sloop, sent to protect the Autumn Isles against French privateers. The water between them teemed with luggers, fishing smacks and bumboats.

It was twilight before the *Whimbrel* reached her berth. It was full dark by the time the travellers found their way through the town's winding, cobbled streets to the Mermaid tavern, which had been Captain Varley's mother's and was now run by his sister, Sal. She looked just like her brother, except she had no golden tooth and far more hair – a crinkly black stormcloud of it, shot through with silver lightnings. When they arrived she was helping a drunken sailor find his way out of the street-door by applying her boot to the seat of his breeches, and she looked quite terrifying. But once the drunkard was disposed of, and Will had introduced himself as a friend of her brother, she welcomed the travellers warmly, and her cooking was as good as Mrs Skraeveling's.

'I didn't think foreign food would agree with me,' said Egg, a few hours later, as he settled himself down on a rug next to the cot-bed where Utterly was to sleep, beside the big curtained bed that was Uncle Will's. 'But that stew was good. I could have eaten more of that.'

'I declare you couldn't, Egg,' said Utterly. 'You had three helpings, and there was none left. Besides, Summertide is not really *foreign*; it is only another of the Autumn Isles.'

'It *feels* foreign, though, don't it? The cliffs are white instead of stone-coloured, and the cows are black-and-white instead of red, and the hills are all round and smooth, like there's no rocks inside of them. It is a soft sort of place.'

Utterly peeked up through a gap in the shutters at the night sky. 'The stars are the same as the stars at home,' she said.

'It is far too late for stargazing,' said Uncle Will, from behind the bed-curtains. 'Go to sleep, the pair of you. We must be up tomorrow at first light, for the carriage to take us to Barrowchurch.'

Egg grunted, turned over, and began snoring almost instantly. But Utterly lay wakeful for a while, glad of those familiar stars, and the faint far-off sounds of the sea.

Those same stars were shining down on Aish, as she went quickly and silently along the high paths of the Dizzard. She had wasted no time looking for Egg at the harbour, for she had guessed where he was before the *Whimbrel* was out of sight. She knew the boy could look after himself. *Perhaps he will look after Will and Utterly too*, she thought, *for in some ways Egg is wiser than either of them* . . . The thought made her smile, and then feel sad, because she loved all three of them and would miss them badly.

Still, she was glad for their sakes they were gone. An uneasy feeling had been growing on her since the wedding. She had felt a strange sense of watchfulness in the Dizzard woods, as if the trees were holding their breath the way small creatures do when a stoat or fox is on the prowl. Unseasonal mushrooms and toadstools had sprouted around High Tarn, and those of her neighbours who had foolishly tried eating them were troubled by dreams of an endless forest and a great black beast that hunted there.

She had watched the little ship till it was no longer even a speck on the horizon, then found a boy to take Will's horse home and set off alone, striding north up the coast past Stannary and Stack and then over the shoulder of Owlsbarrow Beacon to the Dizzard, and her house at Dizzard Tor. There she ate, tied back her hair, and swapped her dress for a short deerskin tunic, which Will and his household would have thought most unlady-like. Then she picked up her long, stone-bladed spear and went down into the woods. A few of her neighbours saw her pass, but they did not speak to her, or offer to go with her. Aish was hunting, and she hunted alone.

The black stag had not come trespassing into her dreams again, but several times in the weeks since the wedding she had sensed its presence. She knew it was not really a stag. It was more like a thought that had focused itself into the shape of a stag, the same way Will Dark could focus a sunbeam through the lens of his magnify-ing glass into a point of brightness so intense that it could start a fire. Only this focused thought was not bright, but black and antlered, with a cold blaze burning in its eyes and magic smouldering off its flanks like black smoke . . .

'What did you need to come back for?' Aish muttered, as she went, spear-in-hand, along the deer-paths and rabbit-runs of the woods around the tarn. 'Are you just jealous? Did you hear my wedding bells, down in that black forest of yours? Is my happiness so hurtful to you that you had to come and spoil it?' She was rehearsing the things she would like to say to the stag if she caught it, although really she was just trying to make herself feel braver. She knew that if she were really to meet it, she might not get a chance to speak at all. For it was very strong, almost as strong and wild and dangerous as the old Gorm, although it was of the land, not the sea. And it had no reason to love Aish.

That was why she had encouraged Will to leave for Summertide, and to take Utterly with him. That was why she was relieved that Egg had gone too. The one thing Aish knew about those eastward isles was that they had lost their magic long ago. The black stag could do her friends no harm there.

At the north-western corner of the tarn, near where the water tumbled out down a series of pretty rapids, there was a cleft between the rocks. It was about the size of a doorway, with a hollow space behind it, which was too shallow to be called a cave. On the rock at one side of the entrance the troll-people of long ago had carved a portrait of Aish herself. It was not a very flattering likeness, for the carvers had shown her as a pear-shaped person with boggle-eyes, but Aish did not mind, because that had been the fashion back then, and she knew they had meant kindly.

Across the opening Aish had tied so many lengths of string that it was hard to see inside. Some of the strings were quite new, while others were so old that they were more moss than string, and looked as if they had grown there of their own accord. From some, holed stones and other powerful talismans were hanging. All had knots in them, which Aish had tied with care, murmuring words of power that would be trapped within the weavings of each knot. The strings and the words and the charms formed a powerful barrier: nothing could go in through the opening, and Aish hoped nothing could come out.

Nothing had come out. The strings were all unbroken, except for a few that had just rotted through and snapped, as string will when it is left out in the weathers for too long.

Aish nodded companionably at her bug-eyed portrait, and squatted down in front of the opening to lean upon her spear and listen. She sniffed the air. She heard only the voice of the water, and the wind in the trees. She smelled only the rich smells of her own woods. There was not a whisper of the one she had come hunting for.

Had she only dreamed him then? Or had he stirred, and sent his dark, stag-shaped thought to seek her out, and then lost interest in her again?

After an hour or more she stood and stretched and went to look downriver. Way off beyond Wildsea's edge, the western sea shone like fish-scales in the moonlight.

'You keep an eye out for him, old Gorm,' she said. 'He is your enemy as much as he is mine. Who knows what he is planning?'

But the Gorm had turned her back on Wildsea, and the sea did not answer. Aish returned to the opening. The moon was higher now, and she could see a second carving opposite the portrait of herself. This second figure was much older, and had almost faded away. It was a crude stick-figure of man. He held a spear in one hand, a curved horn in the other, and from his head grew the spreading antlers of a stag.

7

BARROWCHURCH

The chalk giant had stood upon the steep scarp slope of the down far longer than anyone could recall. The wind blew on him and the snow snowed; the grass grew tall around his chalky outline in summertime and died back again in autumn, and still he stood there. He had seen the broad valley below him change from forest to fields. He had watched Barrowchurch village turn from a huddle of huts beside a marshy river into a neat cluster of cottages and vegetable plots. He had seen Barrowchurch Grange lift proud roofs and tall chimneys, and watched gardens spread around it and an ornamental lake appear in its grounds. He had not seen these sights in any literal way, of course, because he was only an old chalk carving on a hill, and those who carved him all those years ago had not even thought to give him eyes. But he had seen them all the same, and today he saw a little red thing come creeping like a beetle down the white scar of the drover's road on the northern side of the valley.

The red thing was a dusty and slightly battered carriage, drawn by two tired horses, with the crest of the Mermaid Inn upon its door. From its open window, Utterly and Egg looked out across the passing fields and saw the giant.

'Look!' said Egg. 'Some hooligan has scratched a picture of a man on that there hill!'

'The Barrowchurch Giant,' said Uncle Will. 'I have read of him. He is quite famous. No one knows how old he is, nor who carved him there upon the chalk. Summertide people say he is meant to be King Arthur.'

Utterly looked doubtful. 'I don't believe King Arthur would have gone about like that without his breeches on. It isn't dignified.'

'Look,' said Egg. 'Here is the village.'

They looked, but the village was quickly gone again – a few thatched cottages lined up like loaves upon a baker's shelf, an inn called The Stag At Bay, and a very new and ugly red-brick chapel. Then the coachman turned the carriage in through a pair of rusty gates and started up a long drive where bushes crowded in on either side, and weeds were sprouting through the gravel. Utterly, who had been a little nervous about coming to visit such a grand house, was relieved to see how ill-kempt Mr Inshaw's gardens looked. Perhaps she might not be quite so out of place here as she had feared.

'Whoa, there,' said the coachman. The horses came to a stop. Egg opened the carriage door and jumped out, with Utterly and her uncle close behind him. While Uncle Will paid the coachman and helped him to bring their trunks down from the rack on the roof, Utterly looked around.

Barrowchurch Grange was a large, grey house, which had been built in a very fashionable taste perhaps two hundred years before, but now looked old and shabby and uncared-for. All around it the green hillsides swooped up to meet a sky full of low, grey, heavy-looking clouds. Crossing those hills in the carriage Utterly had thought how gentle they looked, as plump and soft as the fat sheep that grazed them. She had liked the way the breeze blew through the grass up there, and the little wheeled huts where the shepherds lived, and how the distant sea made a blue bar along the edge of the horizon. But here in the Vale of Barrowchurch the faces of the hills were steep, and ridged with little grassy corrugations like turf stairs, where even the soil had lost its footing and started to edge downhill. Their lower slopes were gentler, and those were mostly enclosed by fields far bigger than any field on Wildsea, and filled with ripening crops of wheat and barley. Nowhere could Utterly see even a glimpse of the sea, and she wondered if that was why the air here felt so heavy and lifeless. It was so quiet, too. No birds sang. Even the voices of the coachman and Uncle Will seemed muffled.

I do not like this place, thought Utterly. *I do not belong here: I am of the sea, not the land.* But then she remembered Aish telling her she was of the sea *and* the land, and she also recalled that first impressions could be deceptive – she had not liked Uncle Will, or Aish, or even Egg when she first met them. So she resolved to make the best of Barrowchurch.

No sooner had she done so than the front door of the Grange opened and the house began leaking people. There were two footmen in green uniforms who came to gather up the visitors' luggage, several maids who bobbed curtsies, and giggled, and waited to be told what to do, and a stout elderly gentleman who looked so grand Utterly assumed he must be Francis Inshaw and was halfway through her politest curtsey when he introduced himself as the butler, Mr Landover. 'Welcome to the Grange, Mr Dark,' he intoned. His gaze slid over Utterly and Egg, and down to Egg's bare brown feet. He curled one eyebrow into a bushy question-mark.

'This is my ward, Miss Utterly Dark,' explained Will, a little flustered by the questioning eyebrow. 'And this is Egg, our manservant. I mean our boyservant. Our servant boy.'

'I see, sir.' Landover cleared his throat, which magically summoned one of the maids to his side. 'Charlotte, take this lad to the servants' quarters. Harold, show the coachman where he may water his horses. Now, sir, if you and the young lady would accompany me, Mr Inshaw will receive you in the morning room . . .'

'I'll come and find you later,' Utterly whispered to Egg, and then they were each led away in opposite directions, Egg around the side of the house, Utterly and Uncle Will up the steps and in through a large front door.

The Grange was dark inside, and somewhat cavernous, with pillars and statues and suits of antique armour everywhere, and the light gleaming on complicated gilded picture-frames in shady rooms half-glimpsed through open doors. It had the feeling more of a museum than a home, thought Utterly, and rather a dreary, unvisited museum at that.

'Mr William Dark, sir,' said Landover, swinging wide another door. 'And Miss Utterly Dark, sir,' he added, ushering them past him into a room with Turkey carpets on its floor and plump chairs and sofas scattered all about. Large windows looked out upon the garden, but the creeper that grew outside hung so thickly over them that little could be seen of the view, and not much light found its way in.

'Cousin!' said a short, stout man, upsetting a small table in his eagerness as he sprang up from his armchair and came hurrying to greet the visitors. 'Cousin Will! I am delighted – yes, delighted you could come!'

This really was Mr Inshaw, Utterly realized, although he did not look at all as she had imagined him. He had a very round, very pink face, and curly sandy-coloured hair, which he kept trying to tidy by sweeping it backwards with one hand.

'Your servant, Cousin,' said Will, making a little bow.

'Delighted,' said Mr Inshaw again vaguely, and then, gesturing at his sombre, black clothes, 'you find me still in mourning, I fear. Poor Elizabeth . . .'

'My deepest condolences,' said Will.

'She has been gone nearly ten months,' said Mr Inshaw, looking so sorrowful that Utterly was afraid he would burst into tears. But he collected himself, said, 'It is a terrible loss, a terrible loss,' looked all around the room without noticing Utterly at all, and said, 'But is Mrs Dark not with you?'

'I am afraid Aish had to remain on Wildsea, Cousin Francis. I believe I mentioned it in my letter to you . . .'

'Oh, did you?' said Mr Inshaw, looking surprisingly dismayed. 'I must have misunderstood. I thought . . .' He glanced behind him. 'That is, we had particularly hoped . . .'

'It is a great shame,' said a voice out of the shadows in a far corner of the room. A second person stood there, so still that neither Will nor Utterly had noticed him until

49

he spoke. He came forward now. He was dressed all in black like Mr Inshaw, but with a white wig, and white bands at his collar to show he was a man of the church.

'Allow me to present our vicar, Dr Lemuel Hyssop,' said Mr Inshaw. 'A very learned fellow, just like yourself, Cousin, and a great help and comfort to me since Elizabeth was . . . You'll appreciate having another learned fellow to talk to, I'm sure. I declare, I barely know my A-B-C. Dear Lizzie always said I had nothing between my ears but fluff. Hyssop here was the librarian at Lamontane Cathedral till he took a fancy to our ancient church and begged the bishop to let him come and tend to our little flock.'

'Not that the little flock appreciates it,' said Hyssop, bowing to Will. 'Half the village has turned Methodist and would rather hear sermons from ploughmen and travelling radicals at their unsightly new meeting house. The other half tramp over the hill to the church in Swaylebury every Sunday. But I do the Lord's work here, even if no one attends. And, in truth, the lack of parishioners allows me more time for my other interests. I am an antiquarian like yourself, Mr Dark, and there are so many fascinating monuments here in the Vale of Barrowchurch. This must have been a sacred spot long millennia before the church was built . . .'

He spoke pleasantly, but Utterly decided she did not like Dr Hyssop. He was a slim, prim man, with a long pale face and watchful eyes, and a mouth that twisted often into a humourless smile. 'I am delighted to meet you, Mr Dark,' he said, shaking Uncle Will's hand. 'Such a shame your lady wife could not accompany you. I was just this minute telling Mr Inshaw how I looked forward to making her acquaintance. But I see you have brought another lady with you?'

'This is my ward, Utterly,' said Uncle Will.

'Indeed, indeed,' said Inshaw. 'Welcome, my dear.' He ran a hand through his untidy curls and said, 'I confess I am a little unused to entertaining. I have somewhat avoided society since poor Elizabeth was taken from us.'

'If I might make a suggestion, Mr Inshaw?' said Dr Hyssop, who had been watching impatiently. 'Mr Dark and the young lady must be tired after their journey. You should have Landover take them to their rooms. Then, after a little refreshment, I thought we might show Mr Dark the stones. That is the purpose of his visit, after all.'

8

THE CIRCLE AND THE ROW

The servants lived underneath the house, like rabbits in a burrow. The girl called Charlotte led Egg through dim passageways into the kitchen, where a large, cross, bustling sort of person named Mrs Kakewich appeared and told him to sit himself down at the long oak table. Another maid set a cup of milk and a slice of cake in front of him. The housekeeper's name had sounded to Egg like 'Cake Witch', which made him hope the cake would be a good one, but it was just a dry wedge of fruit cake, made with too little fruit, and not a patch on one of Mrs Skraeveling's. He ate it anyway, though. It had been a good while since he had breakfast, and cake was cake.

'*You* shall be sleeping in the cubbyhole under the back stairs, young man,' said Mrs Kakewich. She made it sound as though it were Egg's fault. Her starched white apron looked as stiff as a board, and she wore steel spectacles, and carried a clinking bunch of keys at her waist, like a gaoler. 'It's not exactly spacious, nor exactly comfortable, but it's the best we can do at such short notice. I am surprised your master did not send word that he was bringing a boy with him. But I daresay manners is different on Wildsea . . .'

Mr Landover the butler strode in just then with some complaint about that evening's dinner arrangements, and Mrs Kakewich forgot Egg and went to settle it. Egg felt relieved. This place really was nothing like Sundown Watch. The servants all gave themselves such airs, as if it were a great honour to live in Mr Inshaw's dank old cellar. Even the lowest little scullery maid, who was no older than Egg himself, kept looking him up and down while he ate his cake, like he was something the cat had dragged in.

'Don't you have no shoes?' she asked at last.

'Course I got shoes,' said Egg, through a large mouthful. 'I just ain't wearing them.'

'But where are they?'

'Back on Wildsea, I suppose.'

'Lord bless us!' said the maid.

'I don't like shoes,' said Egg, holding up a bare, brown foot for her to admire. 'Walking's comfortabler without them, once your feet toughen up a bit. You should try it.'

'Lord bless us!' said the maid again.

'What's it like here then?' asked Egg. 'Old Inshaw all right to work for, is he?'

'He used to be,' said the girl. 'Well, his sister did. Miss Elizabeth. She used to run the household, and I liked it better then. We had more to do, and she was a kind lady.'

'What became of her?'

The maid gaped at him. Miss Inshaw's tragic accident had been the talk of the village, and since the maid had never left the village she had never encountered anyone before who had not heard of it. 'She was struck down, weren't she!'

'Struck down? What, by a fit or something?'

'By a thunderbolt! It was in that big storm last October. Poor Miss Inshaw was caught outside in it, and a fearsome great thunderbolt fell on her and burned her all up. They say there was nothing left of her to bury but her slippers and her bonnet-ribbons.'

Egg whistled. He had never met anyone who had met anyone who had been struck by lightning before.

'Since then,' the girl went on, delighted to have an audience, 'Mr Inshaw has turned into a proper old misery-guts. He don't go out no more, and he don't entertain. Before it happened he was paying court to Miss Jane Raftery who lives over at Nutcombe Lodge, but after Miss Elizabeth died he dropped her completely. The only person he ever sees now is that Hyssop that's always hanging round.'

'What's a Hyssop?'

'Don't know much, do you? *Dr* Hyssop is vicar here, though Lord knows why Barrowchurch needs a vicar when nobody goes to the church here, on account of it being stuck up on top of the Knoll, which everybody knows is haunted. But I suppose he is a comfort to Mr Inshaw. I suppose you'd need a bit o' comfort when your sister has been struck by a thunderbolt and blasted into a thousand bits. I mean, there's times I think I wouldn't mind if my sister Rosie was blasted into a thousand bits, but Mr Inshaw and Miss Inshaw was twins, and that means they was closer than what me and our Rosie is, 'tis only natural. But I don't trust that Dr Hyssop. They say poor Mr Inshaw does everything Hyssop tells him. I reckon he's after Mr Inshaw's money, but my dad says that can't be true because Mr Inshaw hasn't *got* no money . . .'

'Hetty Garlick,' hollered Mrs Kakewich. 'If you don't stop spreading rumours about your elders and betters, and start peeling those taters, I'll have your guts for garters.'

'Lord bless us,' gasped Hetty, springing up. 'She means it, too!' And off she scurried.

'And I'm sure you have work to do, young man,' snapped Mrs Kakewich, whisking Egg's plate away before he could finish up the last cake crumbs. 'Won't your master need you upstairs to fetch and carry for him?'

'He ain't my *master*,' said Egg, disdainfully. 'I'm more what you'd call a friend of the family.'

Mrs Kakewich was so shocked at that she could not speak at all, just stood opening and closing her mouth like a beached fish. But Mr Landover, overhearing as he strode through the kitchen, said, 'Friend of the family is it? Well, friend or not, you'll not be going above-stairs without shoes on your feet, and I'll not have you hanging about down here distracting the staff from their duties. So away outside with you, and keep yourself out of trouble till dinnertime, if you can.'

❖

On Summertide, to Utterly's surprise, the foxgloves were white. They stood about in crowds in Mr Inshaw's gardens, nodding their tall spires in the sticky air. They looked like the ghosts of flowers. Uncle Will said it was just the chalk soil that gave them their pallor, and the bees seemed happy enough, bumbling in and out of the pale flowers as if they were no different to the honest, purple foxgloves of home, but Utterly still thought they looked unnatural.

Behind the Grange there lay an ornamental garden, with paved paths and little low box-hedges, and trees clipped into spheres and cubes and pyramids and the shapes of birds, all turning raggedy as new growth blurred their outlines. There was a wide lake, with a Grecian temple on the far shore which would have made a pretty reflection in the water had the day been brighter, and the water not quite so full of duckweed.

'I somehow cannot be troubled to keep the place up,' said Mr Inshaw. 'The gardens were always Lizzie's delight, so I suppose I should keep 'em spick and span in her memory. But Lizzie is gone, and without her, I find it difficult to care. We were twins, you know. Liz is older than me by two full minutes. She *was* older than me, I mean.'

'My brother Andrewe died last year by drowning,' said Will.

Mr Inshaw shook his head sympathetically. 'Do you miss him very badly?'

'We were not close,' said Will. 'But sometimes I read something, or see something, and think, "I must tell Drewe about this." And then I remember that he is gone.'

Mr Inshaw stopped shaking his head and began nodding it. 'I miss poor Lizzie every day,' he said. 'Though Dr Hyssop assures me that we shall be reunited just as soon as—'

'Did our good Lord not say, "Whosoever liveth and believeth in me shall never die"?' said Dr Hyssop, butting in.

'Ah, well, yes, that too,' said Mr Inshaw, and Utterly had the strange feeling that Dr Hyssop's interruption had stopped him from saying something quite different. He nodded a few more times, as if considering the vicar's words, and kicked a small stone into the lake. 'Let us go and look at the Druid stones,' he said.

An overgrown lawn sloped down to the tree-lined River Swayle. A wooden footbridge spanned the river, and on the far side was a meadow where cows had grazed quite recently and left their pats drying in the raggedly cropped grass. Utterly could see where they had trampled the riverbank down to get to the water. The air was full of brown flies. A path slanted across the meadow to a gate in a hedge. Beyond the gate, on the wide expanse of the common, stood the stones that she and Uncle Will had come all this way to see.

There were thirteen of them. They were bigger and paler than the stones that used to stand upon St Chyan's Head, and made from a different sort of stone entirely, pale grey, and pocked with holes like Swiss cheese. In the centre of the circle a number of pits had been dug. Some were shallow, others deep. Some looked quite fresh, with heaps of chalky earth beside them; others were older, and overgrown with grass and weeds.

'Watch where you step,' said Mr Inshaw, stumbling into one of the pits himself. 'Hyssop has been making excavations here, as you can see. He is worse than the rabbits. He has been looking for buried treasure.'

'But finding none, alas,' said Dr Hyssop. 'Although some labourers recently unearthed a small stone chamber over yonder at Nutcombe Lodge, while they were digging Mrs Raftery's garden for her.'

'No treasure in it, though,' said Mr Inshaw. 'Just a blasted great horn.'

'A horn?' asked Will.

'A bull's horn, of prodigious size,' said Mr Inshaw. 'Beastly, ugly thing, no earthly use to anyone, as far as I could see.'

'It was a war horn, or a hunting horn, most fascinatingly carved and remarkably well preserved,' said Dr Hyssop. He glanced at Mr Inshaw as he spoke, and Utterly thought it was a rather cold glance, as though he thought the other man a fool.

'I should much like to see this war horn,' said Will, 'and to know more about the chamber where it was discovered. Could you introduce me to Mrs Raftery?'

Mr Inshaw blushed. 'I am no longer on speaking terms with the Rafterys. There was . . . That is . . . A most unhappy business . . .' He looked miserable for a moment, then brightened as an idea came to him. 'You are welcome to call on them without me, of course.'

'Look,' said Utterly. 'There are more stones.'

From the western edge of the circle two rows of smaller stones led away up a low ridge formed by one of the out-thrust roots of the downs. The stones were almost hidden in the summer grass, but the path they marked was clear enough. Utterly ran along it, with the gentlemen following at a more sedate pace. When she reached the top of the ridge, she saw the stone rows leading on down another gentle slope to where a small church stood upon a steep-sided mound surrounded by dark trees. Beyond the church the hills swept up again and there stood the chalk giant on his down.

'The stone avenue points to the chalk carving,' said Will, joining her at the summit of the ridge and scribbling a sketch-map in his notebook. 'The circle is at one end of a line and the giant is at the other. And in the middle – I take it that is your church, Dr Hyssop?'

'Not at all, Mr Dark: it is God's church, and St Michael's. I am merely their humble servant.' Dr Hyssop smiled his prim smile; it was his little joke, and he had made it many times before. 'The Rectory, where I live, is that house whose chimneys you may see protruding from the trees beyond it. And to the right there, down where the river bends, that other house is Nutcombe Lodge.'

'The mound or hill on which the church stands cannot be natural, can it?' said Will.

'It is called the Knoll,' said Mr Inshaw. 'Local legend has it that there was once a hero who killed a black stag. That may not sound very heroical to us, but I suppose standards were lower in those days, for it was awfully long ago. It certainly impressed the people who lived in these parts, because they made this stag-slayer their king. The Knoll is said to be his burial mound. When we were little, Lizzie and I made great efforts to dig holes in it. I cannot for the life of me recall what we thought we would find – the old king's gold, I suppose . . .'

For a moment, as he recollected it, his face looked almost cheerful. Then he grew sad again. 'I have often wondered if that is why Lizzie ventured to the Knoll on the night of the storm. The wind had uprooted several trees. Perhaps she hoped to find something in the pits where they had stood . . .'

He pulled out his pocket handkerchief, dabbed his eyes, and loudly blew his nose. 'If you don't mind, Cousin Will, I would rather not come with you to the Knoll. It has unhappy associations for me . . . I think I shall return to the Grange . . .'

'Of course,' said Will, and Dr Hyssop agreed that it would be for the best, and they would meet at dinner. Then Mr Inshaw started plodding back downhill towards the Grange, looking so unhappy and defeated that Utterly wished she could think of some way to cheer him up, and wondered if she should go with him. But Dr Hyssop was already leading Uncle Will towards the church, while explaining that it had most probably been built there in an attempt to claim the eerie old Knoll in the name of Christ.

Indeed, thought Utterly, as she went after them, he seemed to know so much about it all that she wondered why Mr Inshaw had needed Uncle Will's opinion too.

9

THE RIVER AND THE OAK

Egg had also been exploring, although he had no guide except his own curiosity. It had led him first to the kitchen garden, and then into the large fruit-cages there, where he ate a number of ripe strawberries and raspberries before a gardener saw him and came running to give him a good hiding. The man shouted loudly enough, but he was old and slow, and Egg outpaced him easily. Still, he reasoned it might be wise not to hang around the Grange until the hue and cry had died down, so he took himself through a hedge or two and across several fields until he came to the river.

He knew this was the River Swayle, which went down to meet the sea at Summertide Town. It was much narrower and more winding in this inland stretch, but just as slow, flowing sluggishly through deep pools overhung with alder and grey willow. Egg pushed his way through the nettles and cow parsley that grew in profusion on the bank, until he reached the same footbridge that Utterly had crossed earlier. He stood in the middle of the bridge to eat the strawberries he had crammed his pockets with before the gardener found him. As he ate, he looked down disapprovingly at the water. Curtains of thick green weed swirled and stretched themselves beneath the surface. It was a lazy, sinister-looking river, he thought, nothing like the quick, bright, lively streams of Wildsea.

He had been standing there for a few minutes when he noticed an eye looking up at him through a gap in the weed. As soon as he saw it, it went away again, but Egg felt it was still watching. He fetched out a strawberry and tossed it into the river a few yards upstream from the bridge. It floated there for a moment. Then there was a sudden swirl in the water and the strawberry vanished. Anyone who had not been paying close attention would have thought a fish had taken it, but Egg had been watching intently, and he knew it had been snatched under by a green hand.

'Magic,' he said to himself, disgustedly. 'I thought this place felt lousy with it.' Aloud, he said, 'I know your game.'

There was a splash behind him. A girl was standing in mid-stream below the bridge with just her head and shoulders poking out of the water. Her long hair was the same sickly green as the weed that swirled around her. Her skin was green too. She smiled unconvincingly at Egg, and he saw that even her teeth were green, like unripe acorns.

'Come swim with me, boy,' she said, holding out a bony hand.

'And get drownded?' said Egg. 'Not likely.'

The green girl scowled. 'You're no fun. I can show you where an otter nests.'

'Go on then,' said Egg. 'I'll walk along the bank. You lead the way.'

'That isn't how it works. You need to come in and I pull you under and then you stay down here for always, and the little fishes nibble your nice bones all clean and white.'

'I don't fancy that much,' said Egg. 'Are you new to this lark? 'Cos you ain't very good at it.'

'I'm not *new*. I've been here since . . .' The girl frowned. 'Since for always, I think. Come swim with me.'

Egg shook his head and threw her another strawberry, but she ignored it and let the slow current carry it past her. 'I could bring you some cake if you like,' he said. 'What's your name, anyway?'

'I do not have a *name*,' the girl said scornfully. She ducked back beneath the water. Egg caught a glimpse of her long green legs as she turned and kicked herself deeper. Downstream, the floating strawberry vanished with a plop. The river flowed on its slow way in silence, even more sinister than before.

❖

If the church on Barrowchurch Knoll had really been built to claim the ancient mound for Christianity, it had not done a very thorough job. The Knoll was much bigger than it had looked from up on the ridge, and the clumsy little flint building with its squat steeple perched uneasily on the top, as if it knew full well it did not belong there. The slopes around it were ringed with ditches in which lay drifts of dead leaves, fallen in past autumns from the tall grey beeches that grew there. There was a heavy silence under the trees, and the strangest feeling of watchfulness and of waiting. Even Dr Hyssop stopped talking as he led the way up the path to the church.

Beside the lych gate the biggest and oldest of all the trees had grown. The biggest and oldest of all trees anywhere, it seemed to Utterly. Its trunk was as broad as a small house. Its huge, gnarled branches were mostly bare, giving it a wintry look. Forests of ferns had rooted themselves in it, and shaggy tapestries of lichen, and clusters of tiny, wet, brown toadstools. There were even other, smaller trees, hollies and rowans, sprouting from leaf-mould and rotted wood in the hollows where its branches joined its bole. Its roots spread down the slope below it like a tangle of tentacles, groping deep into the earth. They were starting to shoulder aside the lych gate, which was leaning away from the old tree as if in an effort to escape. Between some of the roots Utterly noticed stones that were not the white chalk of Summertide.

'It is an oak,' said Will. 'It looks as if has been growing here since time immemorial . . .'

'It is called the Barrowchurch Oak,' said Dr Hyssop. 'It is mentioned in the *Annals of the Isles*, around the year 1020. King Aelfric of Lamontane used to hang traitors from its upper branches, a custom which continued until the sixteenth century.'

'It looks as though someone has tried to burn it down,' said Utterly, who had stepped off the path and gone scrambling over the mass of roots to see the full size of the tree. On its northern side a section of the massive trunk was black and charred.

'It was hit by lightning,' said Dr Hyssop. 'That is why Mr Inshaw did not wish to accompany us. It was upon this very spot that his sister was struck dead. The same storm that battered Wildsea last autumn blew eastward to wreak its havoc on Summertide too. Miss Elizabeth ventured out in it for some reason, and took shelter here beneath the tree. Alas, a bolt of lightning found the upper branches, and the electrical fluid rushed down the trunk and blasted her to atoms. There was nothing

left of her but a few blackened remnants, and some fragments of her clothing.'

Utterly quickly ran back on to the path, in case she had
been standing in the very spot where the poor lady died.

'How awful!' said Will. He felt guilty, for he partly
blamed himself for that storm, conjured up out of the
western deeps by the fire he had persuaded the old sea
witch to light upon St Chyan's Head. It was bad enough
that his meddling had endangered his friends and neighbours on Wildsea, and laid so many of their houses flat; he
had never considered the death and destruction it might
have wrought on other islands. 'No wonder poor Cousin
Francis is so distraught. Whatever can have possessed his
sister to go wandering abroad on such a foul night?'

'Who can say? Miss Elizabeth was a romantically
minded lady. No doubt she thought the tempest and
the lightning blasts sublime, and wished to experience
them at first hand instead of watching through a window
pane. When she realized the storm was moving closer,
she chose to shelter beneath the oak. A most unfortunate
decision. It is dangerous to stand beneath a tree during
an electrical storm, as she discovered.'

'Curious, though,' said Will. 'For I thought lightning is
attracted to the highest point it can find, and the steeple
upon your church is higher than this tree.'

Dr Hyssop shrugged, as if the matter did not much
interest him. 'There were so many lightning-bolts flying

around that night . . . The strange thing is, the tree seemed dead before, but the lightning seems to have revived it. Look.'

He pointed to where fresh green leaves were sprouting from some of the upper branches. 'Hope springs eternal,' he said

But to Utterly the ancient oak seemed an ill-omened sort of tree entirely, growing from an old grave-mound, and capable of summoning down death upon poor ladies who took shelter beneath it. She was glad when they left its shadow and went in through the lych gate to continue their tour. The church was as dull inside as out, and although Dr Hyssop had much to say about its history, none of it could blot out the horror of what had happened to Miss Inshaw. Through the clear faces of the saints upon the stained-glass windows Utterly could see the upper branches of the Barrowchurch Oak spread upon the sky like black antlers.

10

GENIUS LOCI

'There's a girl in the river,' said Egg.

Utterly, who had found her way down to the servants' quarters to tell him of her day, frowned and said, 'What sort of girl?'

'The green sort. I don't remember all the details of her – you know how magic is; trying to remember it is like trying to hold on to smoke. But I was down by the river earlier and I saw her peeking out at me. Hey, did you know? The field beside the river is called Runny Bottom!'

'It isn't!'

'It is, honest!'

Utterly cleared a space for herself on a bench and sat down. They were in the boot room, surrounded by Mr Inshaw's many gleaming pairs of boots and Uncle Will's one rather scuffed and dusty pair, which Mr Landover had told Egg to clean. Egg rubbed half-heartedly at them with a grubby cloth while Utterly pondered what he had told her. She had been hoping to astonish him with the story of Miss Inshaw's fiery death, but it turned out he already knew about that. His adventures sounded far more interesting than hers had been.

'Tell me more about this river girl,' she said.

'Not much to tell,' said Egg, spitting on a boot and rubbing hard. 'She's just some sort of river-Gorm, I reckon, though she's not half as scary as the sea one. She tried to trick me into jumping in and drowning, but I was too clever for her.'

'But Aish said there wasn't any magic here on Summertide,' Utterly objected.

'It's true, Aish did say that.'

'And Aish knows everything about everything. That's what you're always telling me.'

Egg nodded, considering Will's boots from various angles. 'That's true too. But I been thinking. The way I see it is, Aish knows everything about everything *on Wildsea*. But all she knows of other islands is what she's heard from travellers, and maybe they don't know about the magic here, so they never told her.'

'Or maybe the magic here is new,' said Utterly. 'Or – no – what if the magic has been asleep for a long time and now it's waking? Maybe the storm woke it.'

'What storm?'

'The one that struck Miss Inshaw dead. The same one that blew on Wildsea.'

'So it's all the Gorm's doing,' said Egg.

'I don't think so,' said Utterly thoughtfully. 'This place is too far from the sea for the Gorm to care about it. Whatever magic happens at Barrowchurch must be land magic, not sea magic.'

'Do you think Mr Inshaw knows about it?' asked Egg.

'No. Mr Inshaw says he knows almost nothing about anything, and I believe he is right. But Dr Hyssop might.'

'The vicar?'

'Yes, he seems to know a great deal about everything.'

'What's he like?'

Utterly considered for a moment. 'I don't like him,' she said, 'but I am not sure why. Perhaps I'm being uncharitable. He must be a very proper gentleman. They do not let just anyone become a vicar.'

'The servants don't like him either—' Egg started to say, but just then the door opened and Mr Landover looked in.

'Haven't you put a shine on those boots yet, lad?' the butler boomed. 'And begging your pardon, Miss Dark, but you should be upstairs: we shall be serving dinner any minute.'

❖

The dining room was as gloomy as all the rest of Barrowchurch Grange. It was a very large room, with a very long and shining table, and a very grand centrepiece of silver plate in the Egyptian style arranged along the middle of the table. The four diners sat there feeling like lost and insignificant wanderers who had set up camp in the tomb of a Pharoah.

At least, that was how Utterly felt, and she thought perhaps that Uncle Will did, too. But Mr Inshaw seemed to have recovered his composure, and spent a long time telling Uncle Will about the prospects for farming in the area. He said he was thinking of enclosing the common land on which the stone circle stood, and removing the stones themselves so that it could be more easily ploughed.

'My estate manager and my banker both insist it is the only way to make the old place pay for itself,' he said. 'Lizzie would be horrified. She had all sorts of strange fancies that the stones were a fairy ring, and she would not have wished to upset the fairies. But fairies will not pay for new fencing, will they? Or a new roof to the stables? Or wages for all the servants? I fear our late father was not always as careful with money as he should have been, and he left Liz and me with many debts. So if you and Hyssop can't turn up any buried treasure to make ends meet, I suppose I shall have no choice but to plough the poor old common.'

'But then where will the villagers graze their cows and goats?' asked Uncle Will, and they fell to debating politics and agriculture and the rights and wrongs of enclosure, and other very dull things.

From the wall opposite Utterly's seat the late Miss Inshaw's portrait gazed down from a wreath of black crêpe. She looked as though she found it dull too, thought Utterly. She had the same large nose and small chin as her brother, though framed by mousey ringlets in place of side-whiskers. She did not *look* like a person who would have been given to strange fancies. Utterly wondered again what it was that had led her out into the storm.

As if he had read her thoughts, Dr Hyssop smiled slyly at her across the table and said, 'Miss Inshaw told me once that the stones on the common had voices, and they sang to her of things that happened long ago.'

Utterly looked at him, but was not sure if he was joking or being serious. Not certain how he wished her to reply, she said nothing at all.

'You do not seem surprised,' he said. 'You do not say, "Oh, the poor lady must have lost her wits." You seem to think it quite reasonable that stones should sing.' He glanced along the table, as if to make sure that Will and Mr Inshaw were still deep in their conversation. Then he leaned towards Utterly and said, 'Of course, you are used to such things on Wildsea. During my years at the cathedral library I read some remarkable accounts of your island.'

'There are all manner of legends on Wildsea,' said Utterly truthfully.

'But they are not just legends, are they, Miss Dark? Why, I have heard tell how the Gorm herself came ashore on the night of the great storm last year, and how the Hidden Lands were seen, and many other marvels. And what of your uncle's new wife?' Dr Hyssop speared a buttered potato on his fork, popped it into his mouth, swallowed it, and said, 'I understand she is one of Wildsea's original inhabitants, whom the common people term "trolls". Inshaw believes your uncle married her because she owns land in the north of the island and he wants the timber on it, but it is more than that, isn't it? The new Mrs Dark's connexion to the land goes far deeper than mere *ownership*.'

Utterly felt uneasy, talking about Aish in her absence. 'She is a very wise and kind person,' she said.

'As soon as Inshaw told me of her I said, "You must invite this lady to Barrowchurch." I should have valued her opinion on the circle, and the Knoll. It is a great pity she could not come with you.'

'Aish does not care to leave Wildsea,' said Utterly.

'Indeed? How interesting . . .' A second potato followed the first. Dr Hyssop seemed to swallow them whole, like a snake eating eggs. He smiled his thin smile again and said, 'Allow me to help you to some more of this excellent ham, Miss Dark. Have you studied the myths of Greece and Rome, at all? I wonder if you have ever encoun-tered the concept of the *genius loci*, or spirit of place. In ancient times it was believed that every hill, every tree, every river, every rock had its own god or goddess. Every island, too. In our modern age, of course, such beliefs have faded, but what if they were right? What if the tales of ghosts and fairies that persist in out-of-the-way spots like our Autumn Isles are not simply tales but memories of very real and powerful beings who once dwelled upon the earth and in the sea?'

He smiled so encouragingly at Utterly that she began to think she had misjudged him. Suddenly she wanted to tell him everything. She wanted to tell him how the sea had whispered to her when she was little, and how the Men o' Weed had walked, and how on the night of the storm she had gone down in half-remembered dreams that might not really have been dreams into the sea's depths and up onto a strange shore, and met there with a beautiful lady who had called herself the Gorm. And she wanted to tell him there was a girl in the river right here at Barrowchurch, and how she feared the Gorm's magic might have rippled out from Wildsea to wake other magic things on Summertide.

She wanted to tell him so many things that it was impossible to know where to start, and before she could puzzle out how to begin, Dr Hyssop laughed and said, 'Oh, you must not mind me, child. I am just a lonely country parson, who has been educated somewhat beyond his station in life. I have spent too much of my time among ancient books, straining my eyes to read lore that was half forgotten before anyone thought to write it down. It amuses me to let my mind wander down these odd byways, from time to time.'

'Utterly,' said Uncle Will, from the end of the table, 'it is decided: tomorrow you and I shall pay a call on Mrs Raftery at Nutcombe Lodge. Then we shall begin taking measurements of the Druid circle and the stone avenue. Even if we find no buried treasure, at least we shall make a record of the site for future historians, in case Cousin Francis does decide to grub the stones up and plant barley. And you shall help me, Utterly.'

'Of what use can the child be?' asked Mr Inshaw, in a voice that Utterly was not meant to hear, but which she did, because he had drunk a little too much wine and spoke louder than he had intended.

'She can be of every use, Cousin,' said Will. 'When we are at home on Wildsea, Utterly is my Assistant Watcher. Her mind is possessed of an energy not often to be found in one so young. With her help, we shall have your circle surveyed in no time at all.'

11

A FAIRY DIARY

Utterly was almost sure the bedroom she had been given to sleep in had been poor Miss Inshaw's room. It was a pretty room, with pale pink roses on the wallpaper and a view across the river and the common to the Barrowchurch Giant on his hill. There was a large wardrobe with a smell of lavender about it, which, when Utterly opened it, turned out to be filled with Miss Inshaw's gowns. There was a shelf with some books on, a washstand, a dressing table, and a cheval mirror. Utterly stood and looked at her reflection in the mirror for a while before she climbed into bed, thinking how strange it was that the last person who looked into that glass might have been Miss Inshaw herself. Perhaps she had adjusted her bonnet in it before she went out into the storm and got blasted into pieces by the thunderbolt.

That idea made Utterly feel uneasy. She wondered if Miss Inshaw would have minded Utterly washing at her washstand and lying in her bed.

But the knowledge that she lay in a dead woman's bed was not the only thing that stopped her sleeping that night. She would have lain awake for just as long in any of the Grange's other rooms. It was too hot, and far too quiet. Every night of her life until now she had been lulled to sleep by the sound of the sea. Sometimes the sound had been so soft that she had not really noticed it with the waking part of her mind, but it had always been there, easing her into her dreams. Now she was miles and miles from any shore, so far from the sea that she would not hear it even if it rose in another great storm. Here among the downs of Summertide there was only the moonlight, the still, stifling air, the melancholy call of owls in the trees . . .

How did people live at all, so far from the sea?

After an hour or more, she heard Uncle Will's voice downstairs, bidding good night to Dr Hyssop. Then Mr Inshaw must have stepped outside to see the vicar off, for she heard his voice under her window say something she did not catch, and Dr Hyssop reply, 'Don't worry, Inshaw. I will find it, and then we shall go and pay our call upon the Underwoods.' Then Mr Inshaw mumbled something else, and Dr Hyssop wished him a good night. A door closed, and feet scrunched away across the gravel. Utterly wondered idly who the Underwoods might be. She heard Uncle Will come upstairs and go into the room across from hers. And still she could not sleep.

The clouds that had hung so heavy over Barrowchurch all day had cleared away at sundown without spilling a single drop of rain, leaving the sky clear. The moon was almost full, and its ghostly light peeked in around the edges of the curtains. Thinking fresh air might help, Utterly kicked off the sheets and found her way across the unfamiliar room to the window to tug on the tasselled cord that opened the curtains. Silvery moonlight slanted in upon her. Outside, she could see the gardens, and the big fields beyond, and the smooth hills rising darkly all around. The chalk giant on his down looked even taller than he had by daylight.

Turning to go back to bed, Utterly noticed the bookshelf with its little pile of books. Perhaps reading would make her sleepy? The moon did not give enough light to read by, though, so she took down her tinder-box from the mantel and, after a few tries, succeeded in lighting a candle. But when she carried it to the bookshelf she found there were fewer books than she had thought: indeed, there were just three. As the candlelight lapped over the gold lettering on their spines Utterly saw that one was the *Holy Bible*, while another was a dreary-sounding volume called *The Lady's Companion – A Guide for the Fair Sex.*

The third book had no title embossed upon its spine at all, and when Utterly fetched it down from the shelf she found out that it was a journal. The first page was covered with round, childish handwriting, and Utterly had read halfway down it before she realized that the hand doing the writing had been Miss Inshaw's own.

Utterly knew it was very wrong to read other people's private diaries. But was it still wrong if the diarist was dead? She hoped not, for the passage she had read by accident intrigued her, and she did not want to stop. She crossed to the window again, sat down upon the window seat and, setting the candle beside her, began to read.

Tonight, Miss Inshaw had written on the very first page, *I saw again the fairies dancing, out on the common where the old stones stand. They had lit little Lamps, and their Lights moved in circles around the circle of the Stones, and then away, following the Stone Avenue to the Knoll where stands our Church. I am resolv'd not to speak of this to Father or to Francis, for they shall say it is but my foolish fancy. Yet I shall keep it in my Heart, and in this Diary, which I commence this day, 19th September, 1792. E.I.*

That is very nearly twenty years ago, thought Utterly. Elizabeth Inshaw would only have been a girl. And her fairy lamps *did* seem like a foolish fancy, or they would have done to any reader but Utterly. Utterly, however, had read accounts like this before. The old volumes of the Log at Sundown Watch were filled with them; written by Watchers who had seen things they could not explain, and which they struggled to put into words.

Miss Inshaw had not been as careful in her observations as the Watchers on Wildsea were. She had not made an entry in her diary every night, but only when she had something of interest to record. As a result, the entries skipped quickly across the months and years, with Miss Inshaw's handwriting becoming more assured and elegant as she grew older.

Most of the entries were just accounts of the walks Miss Inshaw had taken on the downs, and by the river, and the fairies she had hoped to meet there. She never had met any, but that did not stop her believing in them, for she claimed to have sensed them watching her. *I felt that if I turned, I should see a dear Fairy Child observing me from a Thistle's top. Turn I did, but, alas, not fast enough, so that all I saw was the Thistle bobbing, as though some Sprite who had been resting there had just lately taken flight . . .*

A few months later, after a lot of stuff about how fairies might disguise themselves as sunlit thistledown or autumn leaves, she had written something Utterly did not understand at all: *The full Moon is very bright tonight – it is a Hunter's Moon – and our Giant has his Trumpet and his Spear again.*

The final entry had been scrawled in haste, and the

ink had not been blotted before the journal was shut, so it was smudged and difficult to read. It was not dated, but Utterly guessed it came from the night of the storm last October, for it said: *The sky in the West appears bruised and fantastical, and the Thunder booms like a whole regiment of Cannon. I do not recall the Air ever feeling so heavy before, or the Wind gusting so. Francis says it is but a Storm, but I can feel Magic in the air. I shall put on my coat and walk to the Fairy Hill, to see if the Door is open. Perhaps*

That was all. Miss Inshaw must have intended to finish the entry when she returned, thought Utterly. But she never did return; she went to the Knoll, and there the thunderbolt obliterated her. And now here Utterly sat, reading her final words. *Perhaps* . . . Poor Miss Inshaw! She *did* seem to have been a rather silly person, but Utterly wished she had not been lightning-struck. She would have liked to meet her, and talk to her about the strange things she had seen.

The candle flame fluttered, recovered, fluttered, and went out. A sudden breath of cool air had found its way through a gap between the window and its frame. The curtains stirred gently, while out in the big fields waves moved through the barley and the wheat, all silvered with the moon, so that it seemed the house and its gardens were an island of their own, and all around them a sea of grass was rolling, beating in great breakers against the feet of the downs.

Utterly watched, and as her eyes grew accustomed to the moonlight again she realized that a change had come upon the chalk giant. It was as if the moon, riding high above Barrowchurch, was showing up parts of the old drawing that could not be seen in daylight. The giant was still faceless, but on either side of his head were curving antlers, faintly silver against the darkness of the land. His left hand now held a hunting horn, while his right gripped a straight, upright line almost as tall as himself, topped by a slender leaf-shape.

'Our giant has his trumpet and his spear again,' whispered Utterly. And a cloud hid the moon, and plunged the world outside her window back into blackness.

It seemed the land could be as full of mysteries as the sea.

12

THE DREAMING STONES

Utterly slept deeply and dreamlessly until the gong sounded for breakfast at eight next morning. But the servants had been up for hours by then, cleaning and dusting and preparing the breakfast and polishing the gong, and Egg had risen with them and gone outside before they could rope him into helping with the work.

He had found his way into the pantry first, and helped himself to two large wedges of Mrs Kakewich's fruit cake, which he carried with him down to the river. He ate one for his breakfast, standing on the bridge, but he kept the other in his pocket. The clouds that had cleared away the previous night had returned at dawn, like a thick grey cover laid across the valley to keep the heat in. The river looked sluggish and sullen. The green girl surfaced in the shadows near the bank and glowered up at Egg through a veil of weed.

'What do you want?'

'Brung you some cake, didn't I?' said Egg. 'Just like I promised.'

'I don't like cake,' she said.

Egg shrugged. 'All the more for me then.'

'What is cake anyway?'

'Here.' He tossed the cake to her. The girl caught it, looked at it, sniffed it suspiciously, then looked at it some more.

'It won't bite you,' said Egg. 'It's not the best cake I've ever tasted, I'll admit. The best is Mrs Skraeveling's, but she's way off on Wildsea, so we'll just have to make do with this.'

The girl licked the cake with her long green tongue. She bared her green teeth and carefully took the tiniest bite. She chewed thoughtfully, then ate the rest in two quick, messy mouthfuls.

'Manners!' said Egg warningly. 'You'll get wind, gobbling it down like that.'

'More cake.'

'I ain't got no more. Maybe tomorrow.'

The girl snorted in disgust and submerged, leaving only a ring of spreading ripples on which a few cake-crumbs bobbed.

'Don't mention it,' said Egg. But he didn't mind her

rudeness. Rude, standoffish people interested him. He enjoyed the challenge of trying to butt his way into their favour.

He was already succeeding with the staff at the Grange. Mr Landover actually tousled his hair when he walked back into the servants' quarters, and Mrs Kakewich said, 'I suppose you'll be wanting more breakfast?', which let him know she'd noticed the missing cake.

'You ever heard any stories about that river of yours, Mrs K?' he asked, as he helped himself to toast from the toast-rack and butter from the dish.

'Stories? What sort of stories?'

'Drownings and such?'

'In Barrowchurch? The very idea!'

Egg shrugged. 'And what about that vicar, Hyssop? Why does no one like him?'

'Dr Hyssop is a very learned gentleman,' said Mrs Kakewich primly. 'Even if he has let the old church fall to rack and ruin, and neglected his parish to go fossicking about among those old heathen stones, and even if he does have poor Mr Inshaw wrapped around his little finger. Yes, he is a very learned gentleman, and you'll not hear a bad word about him from me. Now eat up quick, young man: your master's asking for you.'

Egg considered reminding her that Will Dark was not his master, but the toast was too good to waste mouth-room talking, so he let it pass.

❖

There had been a time when Will would have scoffed at the notion of green girls in rivers, but his adventures with the Gorm had changed his views. He might not remember very clearly the things that had happened on Wildsea last autumn, but he remembered enough to be convinced that some power still dwelled out in the western deeps, and that it could not be explained by any of the natural laws he had been taught. And once he had accepted that, it was logical to assume that there might be such powers in other places too; lesser than the Gorm perhaps, but just as far beyond his understanding. So he listened carefully to Egg's account as they walked together through the meadows.

'We know that there was magic on Summertide once,' he said. 'Aish tells me there was magic everywhere once. It is quite possible that the men of olden times built their ring of stones there on the common to channel it, or worship it, or control it, or perhaps to call it back when it began to fade. And I suppose it is equally possible that some lingers still . . .'

Utterly was a little envious of Egg's river girl. She wanted to tell Uncle Will about her discoveries, too: the things she had read in the journal, and the spear and horn she had seen glimmering in the hands of the old chalk giant. But the journal felt like a secret between herself and Miss Inshaw, and as for the rest, here in the lead-grey light of morning she did not feel *entirely* confident it had not all been a dream.

❖

No green girl rose to greet them when they reached the river's edge. They did not cross the footbridge, but took a path that led along the river bank and emerged on the road near the village. There, a stone bridge spanned the river, wide enough for the laden wains to cross at harvest time. On the far bank, with the common and the Knoll behind it, was Nutcombe Lodge.

'It is a shame Mr Inshaw does not get on with Mrs Raftery,' said Utterly, as they crossed the bridge. 'They are such near neighbours.'

'Oh, that is because of the broken-off engagement,' said Egg. 'They told me about that downstairs.'

'You should not listen to gossip, Egg,' said Uncle Will. 'What engagement?'

'Your cousin Francis was engaged to Miss Raftery's daughter Jane, but he changed his mind,' said Egg. 'Last summer they was all ready to announce the wedding, but after Miss Inshaw's accident he changed his mind, and sent a note to say he thought it better if they saw no more of one another. They say it broke Miss Jane's heart. Now her mother won't so much as give Inshaw the time of day.'

'What a shame,' said Utterly. 'I'm sure it would do Mr

Inshaw no end of good to be married. Marrying Aish has done Uncle Will no end of good, he is much more civilized and good-tempered. Uncle Will, you should speak to Mr Inshaw and suggest he makes up his quarrel with Jane Raftery.'

'It is none of our business, Utterly,' said Will. 'And we will not speak of it to Miss Raftery or her mother,' he added, in a warning way. 'Now hush; we are almost at their gate.'

Nutcombe Lodge was not much to look at – it had been an ugly house to begin with, and someone had painted it pink, which had not helped at all – but the gardens would have delighted Mr Skraeveling. They were a paradise of gillyflowers, hollyhocks, Canterbury bells, pinks, daisies, snapdragons, marigolds and flowering shrubs. The blooms were colourful even in the dull grey light of that overcast day, and the air was perfumed with their scents, and loud with the buzz of busy bees. Mrs Raftery and her daughter were busy too, digging up weeds which a boy with a barrow took to a smelly bonfire on the far side of the house. The ladies did not seem pleased to see Will, Egg and Utterly peering over the gate at them.

'You are the gentleman who is visitin' the Grange,' said Mrs Raftery accusingly, pointing her trowel at Will. She rose from the bed of lavender where she had been kneeling, and peered suspiciously at him from beneath her straw bonnet. 'I suppose as that monstrous brute

Inshaw has no time for his own neighbours any more, he is reduced to bringin' in company from outlandish spots like Wildsea.'

'Oh, shh, Mother,' said Jane Raftery, who had come to join her. She and her mother were both short, round ladies, but Miss Jane was prettier, and much younger, of course, and far less angry-looking. She wore her hair in honey-coloured ringlets, which Utterly thought made her look like a friendly spaniel.

'What may we do for you, Mr Dark?' she asked.

Will explained that he wanted to find out all he could about the underground chamber Mrs Raftery had discovered; the chamber containing the antique war horn. He was so polite and so friendly that even Mrs Raftery mellowed a little, and consented to unlatch the gate. While Will, Utterly and Egg followed her across the garden she said, 'It was over here, where my new rose bush stands. That is why I had it dug up, to plant the rose. I thought it was only an old slab of stone, but it took two men from the village a whole day to dig it all out. Five big stones in all, and buried in between them was a prodigious great cow's horn.'

'A cow's horn?'

'Or a bull's perhaps, though it was of such a size as I have never seen on cow or bull. And scored all over with crude patterns, and drawin's of strange creatures, as if a nasty child had scratched 'em there. I would have thrown it away, only Dr Hyssop happened to be passin', and he assured me it was exceedin' historic and philosophical.'

'Do you still have it?' asked Will. 'I should like to see it.'

'I would not give it house-room,' sniffed Mrs Raftery. 'It was a nasty, ugly, dirty thing, was it not, Jane dear?'

'We gave it to Dr Hyssop,' said her daughter.

'How curious,' said Will. 'He did not mention that he had it.'

Miss Raftery had warmed to her visitors enough by then that she offered Will a dish of tea, but he said he had work to do, measuring the stones on the common. Mrs Raftery said it was remarkable the things gentlemen occupied their time with nowadays, there had been none of this measurin' of stones when she was a girl. Miss Raftery, opening the gate to let them leave, whispered that when they saw dear Mr Inshaw perhaps they would pass on her good wishes; she did not blame poor Francis for his behaviour at all, it must be most unsettling to have your sister exploded.

'Well, they are a strange pair,' said Egg, as he and Utterly followed Uncle Will across the common. Utterly wondered if she should try again persuading Uncle Will to talk to his cousin about Miss Raftery.

They walked to the place where the stone avenue crossed the ridge, and followed it eastwards to the circle. There they set to work. They had much to do. Each stone needed to be measured – its height, width and girth.

Then the distances between the stones had to be paced out, and the angles calculated. Drawings of each stone were made – Utterly was good at those – to record its particular shape and markings. Compass bearings had to be taken, and observations to see if the circle or the avenue aligned with any distinctive features of the surrounding hills, or with the places where the sun or moon would rise at the hinges of the year.

While they worked, Utterly thought about how splendid it would be if they actually turned up buried treasure, and could run back to the Grange and tell Mr Inshaw that he need worry no more about money, and would not have to plough the common up. But she knew it was unlikely, for she was constantly stumbling into the holes that Dr Hyssop had dug; they were so many that, if the circle did hide a buried hoard, she did not think he could have missed it. She wondered if it had been the prospect of finding treasure that had made Dr Hyssop so eager to be Barrowchurch's vicar in the first place, and whether, if he found some, he meant to cheat Mr Inshaw and keep it for himself.

But although she did not like Dr Hyssop, Utterly could not believe a vicar could be quite *that* wicked, so she chided herself for being unkind, and concentrated on the task at hand.

The day was very hot, and the slate grey clouds still shed no rain, although they hung so low that their skirts kept brushing against the tops of the downs. It was being so far inland that made her feel pettish and uncharitable, thought Utterly. That was why the air felt so heavy; it had no sea-breezes to stir it about. That was why it was so quiet: there was no murmur of distant waves to break the stillness. Perhaps, when the work was done, she would climb one of those hills and see if she could glimpse the sea from the top of it. Just a distant glimpse would lift her spirits, she felt sure.

But it took all morning just to measure the circle. In early afternoon, before they started on the row, they spread a rug upon the ground beneath the largest stone and ate the picnic Mrs Kakewich had packed for them. Utterly could hear sheep calling to one another on the downs, and the steady drone of insects among the grass.

And perhaps it was the lullaby the insects sang, or the heat, or the picnic lying heavily in her tummy, but she soon began to feel drowsy. And since Egg and Uncle Will seemed to have no inclination to go back to their work just yet, she lay down on the grass and closed her eyes. *Just for a few moments*, she thought. Just a little cat-nap, to make up for her late night . . .

She dreamed that the fields around her, with their rippling waves of wheat and barley, had become a blue-green ocean, and she was so glad to see it that she just floated for a while, rising and falling on the swell, thinking of nothing in particular. Then she noticed a boat was sailing towards her. It was a very small, rough sort of boat, nothing like the *Whimbrel*, and she had a feeling that it belonged to a time when the whole idea of boats had been rather new. It was made from hides stretched over a frame of wood, and its sail was a square of coarse linen, like a big table cloth. At the stern, one of the sailors stood holding a long steering-oar, while his mates busied themselves with the ropes that worked the sail.

In the bows of the boat sat a young man. He did not see Utterly, but she saw him very clearly as the boat sailed past her. She thought he looked a bit like some of Aish's troll neighbours on the Dizzard; the same reddish hair and heavy, handsome features. He wore a white cloth bound around his brow, and somehow, in her dream, Utterly knew this was a sign of mourning, like the black clothes Mr Inshaw wore. The young man had lost someone dear to him, and that was why he looked so sad.

The boat pitched up and down on the steep waves. Foam splashed over the young man, but he sat staring straight ahead, wrapped in his cloak. A great horn lay at his feet, and across his lap was a long thin object, wrapped in deerskins.

13

THE LOST DOOR

Utterly woke with a start. Her clothes were wet, and for a moment she found that perfectly natural, because she had just been swimming in them after all. But no, that had been a dream; the ocean and the passing boat. It had been a nice dream too, though she had felt sorry for the sad young man. She felt sad herself to realize it had not been real, for it had been so good to see the sea again.

Now, sitting up and looking around, she found she could see nothing at all. Everything was white, as if some prankster had quietly taken the world to pieces and sneaked away with it while she was sleeping. Fog, thick and cold, was billowing between the old stones. Utterly could scarcely see the far side of the circle.

Egg, woken by her movements, sat up rubbing his eyes. Together they roused Uncle Will, who took out his watch and frowned at it and said, 'It is nearly five o'clock! I dreamed it was two thousand years ago, and that the Druids were walking in procession around the stone circle, and then marching off along the row. Very stern old gentlemen they were, with flaming torches in their hands, and they were dressed in white bedsheets.'

'There was a fire in my dream too,' said Egg, scratching his head. 'and dancing, and a great black stag . . .'

'I had a dream too,' said Utterly, but when she reached for her memories of it, they were gone. The sea had been in it, and something sad about a boat. How strange – it had all seemed so clear and so very important just a moment before.

Uncle Will rose to his feet and stood blinking at the fog, in which the tall ghosts of the stones came and went. 'This is most vexing,' he said. 'Unseasonal, too. I had hoped to complete our work this afternoon, but now half the day is gone, and we can take no useful bearings in this murk. We shall have to return to the Grange, and resume tomorrow.'

But returning to the Grange was more simply said than done when they could barely see the ground in front of them. 'The circle shall be our compass,' said Will, confidently. 'Our notes will tell us which stone marks the north. If we leave on that side, and strike out down the slope, we shall hit the river, and then it will be easy enough to find the footbridge. And the fog may grow thinner as we go downhill.'

But although it was easy to locate the northward stone, Utterly had the strangest feeling that it was no longer in the same place as it had been when she drew its portrait so carefully that morning. And as they went downhill the fog grew even thicker, until she could barely make out Egg and Uncle Will, let alone tell where they were going.

'We should be at the river by now,' said Egg, his voice oddly muffled by the fog.

'Perhaps we set off at a slant,' admitted Uncle Will. 'But we are still descending; it stands to reason we shall reach the river soon. Aha, there are the trees ahead . . .'

The trees gathered themselves so slowly out of the whiteness that Utterly was almost among them before she realized they were not the willows and alders that lined the Swayle, but the gloomy beeches on the slopes of Barrowchurch Knoll. She stopped walking, and the others stopped too, and they stood marvelling at how far they had strayed from their course.

It seemed quieter than ever beneath the trees. The silence was made somehow deeper by the patter of drops falling from the leaves above.

'Let us think,' said Will, not sounding quite so confident any more. 'If we turn north, we shall reach Nutcombe Lodge . . .'

'But which way is north?' asked Utterly, looking helplessly around at the ghostly trees.

'Why it is to the left, of course . . . no, to the right . . . no . . .'

It seemed so silly, to have become so lost, only a mile or so from the Grange. Egg said they should go back to the circle and start afresh, but Utterly didn't think they could find their way. All of them were growing cold and irritable in their fog-damp clothes.

'We shall stroll up to the church,' decided Will. 'From there a path leads down past the Rectory to the village, Dr Hyssop pointed it out to us yesterday. We shall call at the Rectory on our way by. Perhaps Dr Hyssop will be at home, and can offer us sanctuary until the fog abates.'

But of course they did not reach the Rectory, for as they climbed uphill towards the church the ghostly grey antlers of the Barrowchurch Oak appeared out of the whiteness above them, and Utterly knew suddenly that this was where they had been going all along. The tree's branches seemed to be reaching out through the fog, like gaunt hands waiting to grasp them. And from somewhere beneath it a golden light shone out, like lamplight from an open door.

They picked their way across the slippery lattice of roots, and stood gaping in astonishment. At the base of the oak's trunk a doorway had appeared. It was as if the massive old roots had been drawn aside, revealing two upright stones with a lintel balanced across them and an opening between. Out of this opening shone the golden light; the soft gold of evening sunlight in a summer wood, filtered through layer upon layer of leaves.

'Oh!' said Utterly. 'This was not here yesterday! Not a sign of it . . . Look, there is the scorch-mark on the tree; this hole has opened right where I was standing. But I am sure it was only roots yesterday.'

'A landslip must have exposed it,' said Will.

'Or more bloomin' magic,' said Egg. 'How can there be sunshine on the *inside* of a hill? Specially when we can't see our hands in front of our faces out here.'

Will scrambled closer. He ran his hands over the stones, tracing the curves and spirals of ancient carvings half-erased by time. He ducked into the opening, so that his body blocked out most of the light.

'What can you see?' called Utterly.

Will did not answer, so she clambered up the roots to join him. A smell was coming from the opening; not the musty, dusty smell you would expect inside a burial chamber, but a rich scent of growing things. Uncle Will heard Utterly behind him in the doorway and looked back. 'Stay outside, Utterly. I am not altogether sure . . .'

He seemed to lose track of what he was saying, and his words tailed off as he walked further into the hillside. Utterly did not know what it was he was not altogether sure of, but she was not about to let him venture into the old chamber alone. There was a sound coming from inside the hill now, to go with the light and the smell. It was a soft, steady sighing.

Utterly suddenly felt sure that if she just went with Uncle Will a little way down that bright passageway, she would see the sea, which she had missed so much.

She stepped forward, but before she could pass beneath the stone lintel small, strong hands caught her from behind. 'Utterly!' shouted Egg. 'You don't want to go meddling with whatever's in there!'

'Let me go!' exclaimed Utterly, struggling with him, until they slipped on the damp roots and fell, sliding together a yard or more down the slope. 'Let me go, Egg! Can't you hear it? Can't you see the light?'

'I can,' said Egg firmly. 'And I know there shouldn't be sunshine underground, nor sweet sounds neither. There's magic in there, Utterly, wild magic or worse, and only a fool would stick his nose into it. Talking of which . . .'

He turned, meaning to shout 'Come out of there Will Dark!', but the words faded away before they could find their way out of his mouth. Utterly yelped with shock. In the seconds she had spent looking at Egg, Uncle Will had vanished, and the massive roots of the old oak seemed silently and swiftly to have woven themselves back in place, hiding the stone doorway entirely.

Utterly ran to where it had been, scrabbling at the roots and peering into the dark chinks between them.

'The hill has eaten Uncle Will!' she cried.

It sounded mad. It *was* mad. But it had happened, and Utterly had not one single notion of what to do about it. She stood looking at the place where the doorway had been. Egg stood beside her, likewise at a loss, and all around them on the slopes of the Knoll the ghostly trees regained solidity as the fog blew away, revealing the harebell sky of early evening.

How long had Dr Hyssop been standing there? He was so still Utterly thought he was a tree himself at first, or perhaps a man-sized, man-shaped standing stone, black against the evening light. He moved as soon as she saw him, and came hurrying to where she and Egg waited. Droplets of fog shone like seed-pearls among the hairs of his wig. 'Miss Dark,' he said, 'What has occurred? You seem distressed.'

'Uncle Will is inside,' said Utterly. 'Inside the hill, I mean. A door appeared. It appeared, and then it vanished.'

'He went inside,' said Egg. 'And when we wasn't looking the door just stopped being there.'

Utterly feared Dr Hyssop would accuse them of making up stories, but to her relief he listened solemnly, and showed no sign of disbelieving her.

'So,' he said grimly, 'your uncle has found his way into the Underwoods.'

'Oh, Dr Hyssop,' said Utterly, 'we must run to the Grange and tell Mr Inshaw what has happened!'

101

'Aish'll break her heart in pieces if we don't get him back,' Egg said mournfully. 'He's her husband, and she's only had him a month or two.'

'We shall need men with picks and shovels to break open the hill and fetch my uncle out!' Utterly advised.

'Indeed,' said Dr Hyssop, but he seemed barely to be listening. He was running his hands over the roots where the stone door had appeared, and squinting into the cavities between them, just as Utterly had done. 'Why him, I wonder?' Utterly heard him mutter to himself. 'Why Will Dark, and why now?' Then he seemed to remember her and Egg. He wheeled round to study them, with a look of solemnity that Utterly felt was a mask he had put on to hide some other, more complicated emotion. It was fear, she supposed, although it had looked for a moment almost like anger.

The vicar's voice trembled slightly as he said, 'Children, you are both distraught, and wet with the fog. I shall take you to warm yourselves at my house while I go myself to the Grange and alert Mr Inshaw. Come.'

Utterly did not want to go with him. She did not want to leave the place where the door had been, in case it reappeared. If it did, she thought, she would not hesitate to run inside. Uncle Will had once risked his life to fetch her home from the Hidden Lands, so it was her plain duty to fetch him safe out of the Knoll. But the door had vanished so completely, and Dr Hyssop spoke with such certainty, she decided the best way to help might be to let him take charge.

As they followed him up the path to the churchyard and down another on the Knoll's far side, Utterly said, 'Dr Hyssop, sir, there was a word you used just now: the Underwoods . . . ?'

He glanced down at her as he walked. 'That is my name for the realm your uncle has blundered into.'

'And it is . . . inside the Knoll?'

'Indeed no. The Underwoods are not part of our world at all, Miss Dark. They are another, older world, which lies at angle to ours, and may be reached only through a few secret doorways. There were many such doors once. But one by one the others have all closed. I believe our Knoll may be the very last of them.'

'Then it really is a way into Fairyland? Just as Miss Inshaw thought?'

'I have no doubt that our legends of Fairyland are common people's distorted recollections of the Underwoods. All those dark forests where knights go questing and wicked stepmothers try to lose poor children in old tales, all those places are just memories of the Underwoods. But it is not home to pretty nursery-rhyme creatures with gossamer wings, as foolish Elizabeth Inshaw liked to imagine. It is an awful place, where the great trees riot, and cruel nature is king.'

'Then what is to become of Uncle Will there?' wondered Utterly, growing horribly afraid.

'We must do whatever can be done to save him, child.'

❖

Will squeezed his way along the narrow stony passage that led into the Knoll, and emerged in a wood. For a moment, in his confusion, he assumed the passage must have led him right underneath the church and he was standing on the far side of the Knoll – but that could not be, because he had not walked far enough. Anyway, these trees were older, and more densely entwined than the trees on the Knoll, and it was already twilight in this wood.

He heard Utterly calling his name somewhere behind him. She sounded very far off. He looked back, but saw only the woods, which stretched away from him in all directions. He turned a full circle, searching for the stony passage he had entered by, and by the time he returned to where he started he had forgotten it had ever existed. He could not remember how he came to be in the woods at all, and that troubled him, until he thought about it and realized he must have come here to meet Aish.

Yes, that was it. This was the Dizzard; that gleam of water there between the branches must be High Tarn, and Aish was waiting for him there upon her island on a lake . . . The mere thought of her made him feel braver.

He caught a waft of her musky scent borne on the breeze, and imagined that he heard her singing.

'Aish!' he called, and started running downhill between the trees. But when he reached the water it was not High Tarn at all, just a wide boggy place where ghostly birches grew out of a black mire. Will plunged knee-deep, and stumbled back to firmer ground, almost losing a boot in the process.

So this place was not the Dizzard after all. And now he looked at the trees more critically he could see they were far bigger and far older than the trees that grew upon the Dizzard. Their thick trunks twined and twisted like Chinese dragons, and trees the size of Dizzard trees had taken root in the moss that grew upon them, along with dense colonies of ferns and swaying curtains of ivy and old man's beard and enormous crowds of toadstools. The trees on the Dizzard were ancient, but they were mere saplings compared to these giants. And the Dizzard woods had been home to people for as long as anyone could remember; pigs and cattle grazed in them, the trees provided timber and firewood. Will could not imagine these trees ever allowing anyone to cut or coppice them, or even help themselves to the fallen branches which lay rotting everywhere upon the ground.

The sound he had mistaken for Aish's singing was just a trickle of water spilling into the bog; the scent that had called her lovely musk to mind was only the wild honeysuckle.

'Utterly?' he shouted, dimly recalling that the children had been with him not very long ago. 'Egg?'

'Hssst!' came an urgent voice, out of the shadows nearby.

Will spun around. A figure stood a few yards from him, ghostlike in the deepening gloom. A woman in the tatters of a dress, with wild hair hanging down around her dirty face, and her bright eyes gleaming. 'Come, sir,' she said, 'or he will find you! This is the hour when he comes a-hunting . . .'

At the figure's feet another shape moved; a crouching, hairy thing that bared its teeth and growled and snuffled.

'Come quickly,' whispered the woman. 'We shall keep you from harm.'

Will took one step backwards, then another. He was wise enough to know that there was magic afoot, and that he was being enchanted. Here in these strange woods it was an effort to recall his former life on Wildsea, but quite easy to remember things he had thought forgotten; the Gorm's palace in the Hidden Lands, and how the Gorm had almost drowned him there. He imagined this grey lady of the trees might be some being of the Gormish sort, jealously guarding her woods against mortals in the same way the Gorm guarded her ocean. He took another backward step, then turned upon his heel and ran.

And, once having started running, Will found he could not stop. He was in the grip of the woods and a panic terror was upon him. He felt sure that if he stopped he would hear something chasing him, crashing through the drifts of bracken and the deep entanglements of bramble. He tripped on a briar, fell, rolled, scrambled up, ran on, and glancing back once, thought he saw a shape move across the space between two trees. Was it the grey lady? Was it the creature that had crouched beside her? He did not wait to see, just ran.

Above the trees, the sky was mauve, and deepening into night. The stars that twinkled there were not the stars Will knew. Looking up at them, he tripped again – some fool had strung a rope across the path. He pitched forward, landing hard on a heap of dead leaves. But before he could rise, the ground dropped away beneath him instead. He was scooped up, lifted, and swept towards the treetops in a rustling explosion of leaf-litter. A creaking net of ropes tightened around him till they formed a bag, with Will in the bottom of it, mostly upside down, swinging to and fro like a pendulum ten feet above the ground.

I have blundered into someone's trap, he thought. But whose? The grey lady's? He reached into his pocket for his knife, but it must have dropped out when he fell. The ropes that held him were woody, more like thick creepers than real rope, and he could find no way to break them.

So he dangled there, and he was dangling still when the one who had set the trap came to see what it had caught.

The first Will knew of his coming was a new scent on the air; rank and hot and somehow terrifying. A wide rack of antlers, tangled with dry grasses and dead ferns and trailing tatters of old velvet, moved towards him through the shadows like a dead tree walking. The antlers were almost on the level of Will's head. Below them, a pair of eyes both cold and fiery glimmered with reflections of the stars.

14

THE RECTORY

The Rectory stood at the foot of the Knoll, on its western side. It was a small, flint-faced house, with its gardens much overgrown, and Dr Hyssop lived alone there. It smelled of damp, old books, and mice.

The mice and damp were a bitter reminder to Dr Hyssop of the unfairness of the world. That he, an educated man, a brilliant man, should live in squalor, while buffoons like Francis Inshaw and old fools like his grace the Bishop of Lamontane dwelled in great houses and palaces! But the old book smell was the scent of freedom. For it was in old books, heaped in out-of-the-way corners of dusty libraries, filled with forgotten legends, written in hands and dialects few people nowadays took the trouble to decipher, that secrets dwelled. A man who read those books and traced those secrets to their source might win power and riches befitting his talents. It was things he had read in old books that had brought Dr Hyssop to Barrowchurch. Many an evening he had sat reading in his damp-smelling study, listening to the scratch and scrabble of little claws behind the wainscotting, and smiling his prim smile to himself whenever a snap and a squeal told him that a mouse had sprung one of his carefully laid traps . . .

'You must excuse the clutter, Miss Dark,' he said now, as he unlatched the front door and let Utterly and Egg into the dim hallway. He took off his wig and placed it on a faceless wooden head, which stood upon a table by the door. His short hair was surprisingly red, and it stood up on end like a crop of little flames. 'I have a woman from the village who comes to cook each day, but I dislike maids or housekeepers prying through my belongings, so I manage the cleaning and tidying myself. As you can see, I have been busy with more important matters lately.'

The house was a magician's cave, lined with shelves that sagged beneath the weight of the books they held. A stuffed owl in a case regarded the visitors with a look of disapproval. In the drawing room, glass-fronted cabinets held more dead birds and animals, and a collection of stones and other curios. Dr Hyssop told Utterly and Egg to sit, disappeared into the back of the house somewhere, and returned with two cups of milk and a plate of bread and butter.

'Thank you, sir,' said Utterly and Egg.

Hyssop smiled at them. 'Wait here for me,' he said. 'I shall go down to the Grange and return with Mr Inshaw and a few stout fellows with spades.'

'Oh, please be quick, sir!' said Utterly, feeling terribly afraid for Uncle Will.

'It will not take me above half an hour,' Dr Hyssop promised, closing the door behind him.

An instant later, just as she was turning her attention to the bread and butter, Utterly heard the small, definite sound of a key turning in the lock.

She ran to the door and tried the knob. 'He's locked us in!'

'Why would he do that?' asked Egg. 'You are turning it the wrong way, I expect, or pulling when you should be pushing, let me try . . .'

But the door was indeed locked. Egg banged on it with his fists and shouted, 'Hoy! Vicar!' while Utterly went to the windows. Those, too, were locked, and there were metal bars on the outside, painted white to match the woodwork. (One of the previous vicars had been much alarmed by news of the revolution in France, and had fortified the house against rampaging mobs.) As Utterly was trying the window catches she saw Dr Hyssop go striding past outside. She knocked on the glass to draw his attention, and shouted his name several times, but he seemed afflicted by a sudden deafness. He did not so much as glance at her, just put his wide black hat on and hurried out through the front gate, vanishing from sight behind the overgrown hedge.

'Perhaps it was absent-mindedness,' she said. 'Vicars are often absent-minded. Reverend Dearlove once walked halfway to Stannary in his nightcap when he was pondering ideas for a sermon. I expect Dr Hyssop is contriving ways to rescue Uncle Will, and in his distraction he simply locked the door behind him out of habit.'

'If he was in the habit of locking it,' reasoned Egg, 'then it would have been locked when he let us in. Which it weren't. No, he's up to something, that one, and I don't like it. Why didn't he tell your uncle Will about these so-called Underwoods before? Why didn't he warn him? How long had he been stood there watching when we saw him? I bet he saw your uncle go blundering in through that stony doorway and didn't lift a finger to try and stop him. Oh, he's plotting something all right.'

Utterly did not want to believe him, but she could not deny that there was something very strange about Dr Hyssop's behaviour. And as she looked around the room she could not help but notice the dirtiness of his home, and all the strange artefacts he had amassed – the skulls and fossiliferous remains, the articulated skeleton of a snake, prints of Druidical-looking gentlemen performing odd rites in rustic temples, and a little wizened scowling thing that she suspected might be a shrunken head.

'It is all so unlike the home life of our own dear vicar,' she said. 'You wouldn't catch Reverend Dearlove collecting shrunken heads and pictures of odd heathen goings-on.'

'That's 'cos Reverend Dearlove is a proper gentleman, and this Hyssop's a wrong 'un,' said Egg.

'I do not like him either,' said Utterly. 'But at least he has gone to fetch Mr Inshaw . . .'

'So *he* says. He's probably gone to tell him we've all fallen down a hole. Then he'll come back and drown us in the well.'

'Oh, Egg, he wouldn't! Would he?'

'I don't know what he'd do, and I ain't a-waiting here to find out. We've got to get out.'

'But what about poor Uncle Will? How can we help him?'

'I don't know. But we ain't no use to him shut in here.'

Egg tried the windows, although Utterly had told him they were locked, and the bars outside meant there was no point in breaking them. He tried the door again. He wasted twenty minutes or more trying to loosen the hinges with the butter knife, while Utterly opened the cabinets and rummaged among the bones and curios there for anything that might be used to prise it open. There was nothing. 'We must wait, and hope that we are wrong, and pray that Dr Hyssop returns soon with Mr Inshaw,' said Utterly at last.

But Egg was not listening. His gaze had settled on the fireplace.

'We can get up the chimney,' he said.

'I am certain we cannot.'

'In London and places they send kids up chimneys to clean them. Your uncle told us all about it.'

'Yes, in order that we might learn what an abominable practice it is, and how often the poor unfortunate little chimney-sweeps get stuck halfway up and perish miserably. *I* don't want to perish miserably, Egg.'

Egg snorted, eyeing up the chimney breast. 'Those were London chimneys he was speaking of. This here's a proper big old country sort of chimney. I reckon we could climb up it easy. I used to climb all over the sea cliffs at Stack looking for bird nests, and they are higher than any chimney.'

'But Egg, *I* did not used to climb all over the sea cliffs at Stack . . .'

'You'll soon get the hang of it, Utterly. It's just a matter of finding where to put your hands and feet, and remembering not to fall off.'

Egg was already in the fireplace, reaching up to shove the metal damper out of his way. There was a rushing, scampering sound as a torrent of soot came down on him. The soot spread out smokily into the room, thickening the air, making Utterly cough and back away. Egg was coughing too, but the sound was oddly muffled by the chimney. 'It ain't too bad,' he called. 'You brace your back against one side and kind of walk up the other. Come on.'

More soot came down, with a rustle and a whoosh. It burst from the fireplace in a greyish cloud and settled upon the hearth rug, the furniture, the half-eaten slabs of bread and butter on their plate. It made a horrid mess, but Utterly told herself that was Dr Hyssop's own fault for locking people in, and for not having his chimney swept more regularly.

She tried to calm herself. She thought of the sea, and the soft, sleepy sounds it made on the shingle below her bedroom window at home when the tide was high and it was in a gentle mood. She made herself match her breathing to the slow rhythm of the waves. Then she stepped into the fireplace, where she could hear Egg scrabbling and coughing somewhere high above her. Keeping her eyes shut as much as possible against the steady rain of soot, she started to scramble up through the narrow gap between the brick of the chimney breast and the metal of the damper.

But she had not yet found her way past the damper when she heard voices outside in the garden. The first voice was Dr Hyssop's, saying something she did not catch, and the second was Mr Inshaw's, asking loudly, 'But why keep the children here? Why not let them come back to the house?'

'So they could tell all your staff what has befallen

Dark?' said Dr Hyssop, snappishly, and apparently just outside the drawing-room window. 'No, I mean to secrete the brats here until . . .'

His words blurred as he went into the porch. Utterly called up the chimney, 'Egg! He's back!'

'Hurry then!' came Egg's voice, accompanied by another avalanche of soot. 'I'm nearly out!'

But the front door banged, and then a key turned in the lock of the drawing-room door. Utterly lost her footing, slipped, and dropped down into the fireplace just as the vicar rushed into the room. He snatched hold of her arm and dragged her out of the hearth, shouting, 'Watch her, Inshaw! Don't let her escape!'

Mr Inshaw filled the doorway, looking in shock around the soot-filled room, then down at Utterly. 'Where is the boy?' he asked.

Dr Hyssop leaned into the fireplace and shouted angrily, 'Come down here, sir!'

'Not – *something* – likely!' came Egg's voice, very dimly, from on high. (The *something* was inaudible, and Utterly thought that was probably for the best.)

Dr Hyssop started to bellow some choice phrases of his own, but at that moment a clotted mass of soot and old bird's nest dropped down the chimney and burst upon his face. He reeled out of the fireplace choking and cursing, looking as if he had just emerged from a long day's labour down a coal mine.

From outside the house came the sound of something breaking. Dislodged roof-slates began dropping past the windows like bats. Barging past Utterly, Dr Hyssop thrust Mr Inshaw out of his way and with a shout of, 'Watch her!' went rushing out into the garden.

Utterly tried to go after him, meaning to stop him harming Egg. But Mr Inshaw blocked the doorway again, and when she tried to push past him he took her small hands in his large ones and held her easily. 'Please, control yourself, Miss Dark,' he said.

'Oh, Mr Inshaw, let me go! Uncle Will is lost inside the hill and we must rescue him! Let me go!'

'Utterly, I cannot.'

Utterly kicked his shin and writhed her hands free, but there was no way past him. She ran to the fireplace instead and shouted up the chimney, 'Egg! Mr Inshaw and the vicar are in league! Run!' Mr Inshaw had hold of her again. 'Run, Egg! Run! Fetch help!'

Egg had been having a disagreement with the chimney-pot. It was a stubborn, terracotta affair, mortared in place on the top of the chimney stack and far too slim for even him to wriggle up. But the mortar was old and crumbling, and a few hearty shoves were enough to send the pot crashing down to shatter on the ground below. Egg stuck his sooty head out into clean air, and was greeted by a weathervane in the shape of a running stag. It squeaked on its fixings as he grabbed hold of it to pull himself out of the chimney. Crouched on the top, he turned to catch Utterly's hand and help her up, for he was sure she would not be far behind.

All he caught was her voice, echoing up the chimney from below. 'Egg! Mr Inshaw and the vicar are in league . . .'

He froze for a moment, not wanting to leave her behind. Should he go back down and help her fight her way out? But he could be no use to her if he let himself be captured too.

The sounds of a brief struggle came up the chimney, then Utterly again: 'Run, Egg! Run! Fetch help!'

That made up Egg's mind for him. He jumped down onto the roof, meaning to edge along it to the far end of the house. But the roof was steeper and slipperier than he had reckoned on. After a few steps he found himself slithering downwards, upright at first, then sitting, then flailing wildly for a handhold until he shot over the eaves in a clattering rush of dislodged slates.

His fall was broken by Dr Hyssop. The vicar had come running out of his house a moment earlier, and Egg landed on him like a well-aimed sack of coal. Dr Hyssop went down in a cloud of soot, with Egg on top of him, and slates falling and shattering all around. They were both stunned, but Egg recovered first. He sprang up, shaky but unharmed, and looked at the house, wondering if there was yet some way he could get Utterly out of it. But Hyssop was struggling to his feet with a wicked look in his eye, and Utterly's words were still in Egg's head.

Run, Egg! Run! Get help!

Egg ran. Across the ragged garden, through the bean-rows of an abandoned vegetable plot, over a broken-down fence, and uphill into the trees upon the Knoll.

'Hellfire!' roared Dr Hyssop, crashing back into the house.

It was most unsuitable language for a vicar, thought Utterly. But then Dr Hyssop was turning out to be a most unsuitable sort of vicar entirely. He came into the drawing room and stood and scowled at her. He had torn off his collar, and in the opening of his shirt she saw a small jawbone, a weasel's perhaps, strung on a leather cord and dangling around his neck. His face was flushed, his eyes feverishly bright, his hair a stubble-fire. Utterly stood and glared at him while Mr Inshaw held her gently but firmly by both arms.

Dr Hyssop said, 'No doubt you think your little friend is very clever, Miss Dark, but I shall have him yet.'

'Now listen here, Hyssop,' said Inshaw. 'I'm not at all

119

clear what's going on. The doorway to the Underwoods has come open again, you say? And Cousin Will has wandered in and got himself lost? But why do we need to keep these poor children captive?'

'Because if we don't, they will run straight to your servants, or the villagers, and start telling them what has happened, and before you know it, you will have half Barrowchurch up here with picks and crowbars trying to tear down the Knoll!'

'Well, I have always said we should try breaking the Knoll open . . .'

'You fool,' snapped Hyssop. 'This is why you should stay silent, and let me think and speak for you. Don't you see? *Digging may destroy the door.* The door is our only way into the Underwoods, and it opens only for those it wishes to admit. That boy will be halfway to the Grange by now . . .'

An idea struck him; a grim idea, to judge by the look upon his face. He fetched down a mahogany box from one of the shelves and unlocked it with a small key from his waistcoat pocket. Inside lay two long-barrelled pistols with their polished wooden handles gleaming like new conkers.

'I was considered quite a decent shot at Cambridge,' said Dr Hyssop, taking the guns out. 'I once killed a fellow student outright in a duel on Grantchester Meadows. Put a ball straight through his heart from a distance of twenty paces.'

'Now steady, Hyssop,' said Mr Inshaw, pleadingly. 'This is just a boy we're dealing with . . . A frightened child. You only mean to scare him, I am sure. You do only mean to scare him, don't you, Hyssop . . . ?'

But Dr Hyssop turned and strode from the house without another word, slamming the front door behind him.

Mr Inshaw shook his head. He kept hold of Utterly, and his grip was firm, but he was careful not to hurt her. 'I am sorry, child,' he said. 'When I asked Cousin Will to come here I little realized – I did not know that he would bring you with him, or the boy.'

Utterly said nothing. She thought of poor Uncle Will, lost and alone in the otherwordly wood. She was very disappointed in Mr Inshaw.

'You must understand,' he went on. 'I never wanted any part in Hyssop's schemes. All I want is to free my poor, dear sister.'

Utterly twisted around so she could look up at him. 'But Mr Inshaw, I thought your sister was dead?'

From outside somewhere came the sudden, startling crack of a pistol.

15

THE RIVER'S EDGE

Egg was halfway across the common when the first shot rang out. He had thought of making for Nutcombe Lodge, which lay so much nearer than the Grange, but Mrs Raftery had struck him as unfriendly. Egg did not think she would believe him if he went barging into her house with his tale of villainous vicars and man-eating hills. So he was heading for the Grange instead, running along the avenue between the twin rows of stones. He had not won over Mrs Kakewich and the other servants wholly, but he had been working on it, and he thought they would at least give him a fair hearing.

He was halfway to the circle when one of the stones exploded as he passed it. Or did not explode exactly, but sparks flew from it, and quite large splinters, one of which stung Egg on the cheek. The clap of the pistol-shot, arriving a moment after the ball, explained things. Somebody was shooting at him, and Egg had a good notion as to who that somebody might be.

The harebell colour of the evening sky was darkening to some deeper blue Egg didn't know a name for. A saffron moon was lifting from behind the hill where that old chalk giant stood. It cast enough light that he could see Dr Hyssop striding towards him from the Knoll. As he watched, the vicar stopped, and a sudden white cloud obscured him. A second pistol ball flicked through the weeds ten feet from where Egg stood, taking the top off one of those ghostly white foxgloves.

Which was not bad shooting at all, in that failing light and at such a distance. A man who owned a brace of pistols and could shoot them so well probably knew how to reload them in a hurry too.

The Grange suddenly looked impossibly far away. Nutcombe Lodge was nearer, but Hyssop could easily cut him off if he made for it. Egg looked left and right for shelter. The nearest place on the wide bare common where he had a hope of hiding was the line of trees beside the river. He took off downhill towards them, crashing through nettles and waist-deep grass. A pistol barked behind him, but the ball missed him by a wide enough margin that he never heard where it went.

Which don't mean the next one will miss too, he thought grimly.

He thundered downhill through the last strands of mist and plunged into the trees, then down the crumbling bank into the river. It ran shallow here, west of the footbridge. Egg waded across it and found deeper water under the willows on the far bank. Half-swimming and half-walking, he struck out downstream. He was twenty yards away, hiding in a clump of bullrushes, by the time Dr Hyssop appeared. The vicar poked with his shoe at the bit of bank Egg had stumbled down, then stood looking up and down the river for a sign of him.

Well this is a fine how-d'ye-do, thought Egg. How was he supposed to help Utterly and her uncle now? He sank deeper, soft river mud squeezing up between his toes, till the water was almost up to his nose. Dr Hyssop moved slowly along the bank. 'Oh, boy,' he called, in a wheedling sort of way. 'Oh, "Egg", if that is indeed your name . . . Come out so we can talk this over, man to man. I'll put away my gun. It was only loaded with salt, anyway. I just meant to frighten you . . .'

But he had two guns, not one, and he had not put either of them away; Egg could see them in his hands as he prowled to and fro, with the moon gleaming cold upon their barrels. So Egg kept to his hiding place, and held his tongue, and watched the vicar prowl till the shadows among the trees downriver hid him, and then listened till

124

the sounds of his sneaky footsteps faded away, and even then he stayed as still and quiet as he could, although he was starting to shiver a bit by then, and his teeth were inclined to chatter.

'Did you bring me any cake?' said the river girl. She had surfaced so quietly beside him that Egg did not know she was there until she spoke. The shock of it made him swallow quite a bit of her river.

'No I didn't bring you no cake,' he spluttered. 'And if I had it would be all wet and spoiled, seeing as how I've been underwater this past half hour. I got better things to think about than cake! That vicar's nabbed Utterly Dark, who's a good friend of mine. I've got to think of a way to get her back.'

The green girl watched him. Her eyes in the gathering dusk shone with a faint inner light, green as the rest of her. This was the moment of truth, Egg supposed. If she decided to drown him she could probably do it; he was weak from the chase and cold from the river, and he reckoned those spindly hands of hers were stronger than they looked.

She snorted. 'You can't get her back. Old magic is stirring. You can't fight that. No one can.'

'It's the vicar I want to fight,' said Egg. His breath came in shivery gasps. Was this the river girl's plan? To keep him talking here until he froze and sank? 'That vicar and Mr Inshaw. Utterly reckons they're in it together.'

The girl shook her head. 'It is not them you have to fear. It is the Hunter.'

'The who?'

'The Black Stag. He walked in the first woods when the world was young. He has been sleeping a long time, but now he's restless. The big storm woke him. Soon, when he has his spear and his horn again, he will arise and hunt.'

'There's altogether too much hunting going on round here for my liking,' grumbled Egg. Reluctantly, he squashed his hopes of getting back to Hyssop's place and setting Utterly free. 'I got to get to Summertide Town,' he decided.

'Why?'

"Cos from there I can get to Wildsea, and Aish is on Wildsea and Aish'll know what to do. Maybe I can work out a way to bring her back with me. Aish'll be a match for Hyssop and Inshaw. And she could handle this Hunter of yours any day, I reckon. She'd like to meet you. You'd like her. I could bring you some of Mrs Skraeveling's cake from Wildsea, too. Mrs S makes better cakes than any you'll find here. Best cakes in the whole world, prob'ly. But I need to get there fast.'

'Fast,' said the girl, and giggled.

'Yes, fast. Do you know what that even means, in this lazy old river?'

The girl stopped giggling. Egg wondered if he had offended her. But after a moment she said, 'There is a

126

boat tied up beyond the alders there. You'll need a boat, if you want to go *fast*.'

Egg couldn't see the boat. He couldn't even see the alders. But he let himself float downstream, and the moon poked a few of its quicksilver fingers down between the branches until one rested upon an old punt tied up to a post on the bank. Egg scrambled aboard, shivering. He was glad to be out of the water, but a lot came into the punt with him, and a lot more oozed up between the planks as it took his weight and settled deeper into the river. It was not much of a punt, just an oblong of half-rotted planks with a low rim around them and a rusty bracket on the front end where a duck-gun could be mounted. There was no oar, but a long pole lay among the dead leaves on the bottom boards.

Egg fumbled with the mooring rope, but the knot was tight and his fingers numb. He fetched out his pocket knife and cut the rope, though it was a sin to waste good rope. Then he looked around for the girl.

'What now?' he said.

But the girl had gone back down into her depths, and did not answer. Egg was alone again. The river flowed past, carrying its reflections of the moonlight carefully, as if it were afraid of spilling them. Egg let out an exasperated sigh.

From upstream somewhere, like an echo or an answer, came another sigh. It grew into a hissing, that turned into a crackling, that turned into a roaring. Egg crouched in the punt, knife in hand. Between the trees, something showed white.

'Oh no!' said Egg.

The wave rounded the bend of the river and rushed down on him. A wall of white water, marbled with moonlight, churning with fragments of torn-off branches. It struck the punt, lifted it, and swung it out into midstream, half-buried in foam, barrelling downstream towards the next bend. Egg clung to the seat, the sides, the old gun-bracket, anything he could grab a hold of as the boisterous river flung him about. He saw the lights in the windows of Nutcombe Lodge gleaming in the flood as he was swept past Mrs Raftery's garden. He plunged through the thick shadows under Barrowchurch Bridge and out again into moonlight. The green girl sported in the punt's bow-wave, appearing now on this side, now on that, just like the dolphin that had played around the bows of the *Whimbrel*.

'Is this fast enough for you, boy?' she shouted. But it was hard to hear her over the wilder shouting of the water and Egg's open-mouthed, unending wail of terror.

16

THE LEGEND OF
THE HUNTER

Mr Inshaw had decided the soot-covered drawing room was not a suitable place to await Dr Hyssop's return. Or perhaps he was afraid Utterly would try to escape up the chimney again. He marched her across the hall and into Dr Hyssop's study, where there was no fireplace at all, only a stove. She sat there miserably on a hard chair, worrying about Egg and Uncle Will. Outside the window the moon was rising, like a huge balloon breaking free of the skyline above the chalk giant's head. It looked as if it were made of yellow silk and the Man in the Moon had lit a cosy fire inside.

'Hyssop has gone too far this time,' muttered Mr Inshaw. 'He is behaving like a brigand, or the wicked uncle in a play. I regret it exceedingly.'

'Then why are you helping him?' asked Utterly.

'For my poor sister's sake, of course!' said Mr Inshaw, very loudly and a little irritably. He looked at Utterly then. She saw that he was frightened, and angry, and ashamed.

'It is for Lizzie's sake,' he said, more softly. 'She was not really consumed by lightning, you see. That is just a tale Hyssop devised to explain her disappearance. He said if I told the truth, people would say I was a lunatic, and might even think I had done away with Lizzie myself. So he scorched the old oak with gunpowder from those duelling pistols of his and put about a story it had been struck by lightning. So many trees were struck during the storm, it seemed perfectly likely . . .'

He fell quiet, and Utterly could think of nothing to say, so they sat in silence for a while. Then Mr Inshaw said, 'Barrowchurch has always been a troubled place. There was legends of ghosts and fairies and black dogs and Lord knows what other goings-on, even when I was a boy. But until last autumn it was possible to believe it was all no more than old wives' tales. Then something changed with that blasted hurricane, that tempest off the western sea. Lizzie said there was magic in the air that night. She had always had a sense for it. She said it was because she took after our mama, who was a Dark from Wildsea, where people still believe such things. I suppose that is what led her outside into the storm, while I closed my shutters on it and went to bed . . .

'When I woke next morning the wind was still wild and a dozen trees were down and they told me Lizzie had not come home. I went out searching for her, and there was the stone door, and inside it that . . . other place, the place that Hyssop calls the Underwoods. Then the door vanished as if it had never been. Hyssop says it opens only for those it chooses. It chose my sister, for some reason. Now it has chosen your uncle.'

Utterly frowned. 'How does Dr Hyssop know all this?' she said.

'Ah, well,' said Mr Inshaw, looking very distressed, 'that is the strangest part . . .'

'Dr Hyssop knows it because he has studied it for many years,' said Dr Hyssop's own voice, and Utterly turned to find him standing in the doorway.

'Hyssop!' said Mr Inshaw, springing up. 'What happened to the boy?'

Dr Hyssop shrugged. 'I have no idea. It is horribly dark under those trees, and the boy has that animal cunning one sometimes meets with in the lower orders. Perhaps he has drowned. Perhaps he has escaped. But it's of no consequence. I fancy he will not dare to show his face in Barrowchurch again.'

'And what if he makes it to Swaylebury, or Wavering, or Summertide Town, and raises a hue and cry against us, Hyssop?'

'Good luck to him! A barefoot vagrant slandering a

respectable landowner and a member of the clergy? They will throw him straight in the town gaol.'

'But the whole district must have heard you shooting off your blessed pistols . . .'

'And the whole district will think some honest yeoman is out shooting rabbits on the common.' Dr Hyssop set the pistols down on his desk and fell heavily into an armchair. A small cloud of soot rose from his clothes. 'What I still don't understand is, why did the stone door open for Will Dark?'

'Was that not your plan, Hyssop? Was that not why you encouraged me to invite the poor fellow here?'

'Not at all. Will Dark is nothing. When I told you to fetch him here I was hoping he might bring his wife, the troll-woman. She has some primitive magic about her, from what I can gather. I hoped she would help me find what we have been seeking.'

'Perhaps some of her magic has rubbed off on Cousin Will, so to speak,' said Inshaw. 'Or perhaps he had some already – he is a Dark, you know. Oh, do not glower at me so, Hyssop. I am tired of you treating me like a fool! I may not be an educated fellow like you, but I do my best. All I want is for poor Lizzie and poor Cousin Will to be restored to us safe and sound.'

'That will not happen unless I find what I am seeking,' said Hyssop sullenly.

'And what is that?' asked Utterly. 'What is it you wanted Aish to help you find?'

Both men turned to look at her. They were the kind of men who easily forget that children exist. Until she spoke, they had utterly forgotten Utterly.

'There is an ancient legend about this place, Miss Dark,' said Dr Hyssop. 'It has faded from the memories of the common folk, and their betters never knew it, but I found a version scribbled in pig-Latin in an ancient manuscript in a forbidden vault of the cathedral library on Lamontane. It tells of a time so long ago that there was no barrier between the Underwoods and our own world, which was all forest too in those days. A Hunter ruled those forests, and he ruled them by fear. He was not a man, but one of the ancient powers of the Earth. He carried a spear that could strike down any that dared challenge him, and a horn that summoned his pack of phantom hounds. But one day a young man crept up on the Hunter while he slept, and stole the horn and the spear. Since the spear held part of the Hunter's own strength, he was weakened without it. He could no longer return to our world, and he fell into a long sleep, imprisoned in the Underwoods . . .

'But lately he has been stirring. He is still too weak as yet to pass through the stone door into our world. He needs his spear. He needs his horn, that he may summon up his hounds . . .'

'So Hyssop reckons that if we return the horn and spear to him, this Hunter fellow will restore Lizzie to us,' said Mr Inshaw.

'Indeed.' Dr Hyssop scowled at him, annoyed at having his story brought too hastily to an end. He opened a drawer of his desk and took out something: a huge, curved horn, yellowish in the lamplight like old ivory, and covered all over with crudely carved patterns and drawings of strange animals. Utterly saw a deer there, and what seemed to be a hairy rhinoceros.

Dr Hyssop laid the horn down carefully beside his pistols. 'The horn has already been discovered, as you see. Mrs Raftery called me to see it when her men dug it up, "because I know you have an enthusiasm for these grubby old relics, vicar". Ridiculous woman. She let me take it away without ever guessing what power it holds. But where is the spear? That is the question. I have dug into the sides of the Knoll; I have sunk holes among the stones on the common, but I have found no trace of it. Which is why I hoped the new Mrs Dark might come and use her skills to tell me where it lies . . .'

Utterly did not think Aish would have helped Dr Hyssop. She did not think Aish would have liked him at all. And she did not understand how he knew so much about who this Hunter was and what he wanted and what he would do in return for his spear and horn. She suspected it was all just a theory, like the clever theories Uncle Will had about the Gorm when he first returned to Wildsea. And, as Uncle Will had discovered, clever theories were not much use for understanding magic . . .

But then she remembered that Uncle Will was trapped in the Underwoods, and it occurred to her that, if Dr Hyssop was right, the Hunter might let him out, if only she could find his spear for him.

'The chalk giant has a horn and spear,' she said.

Dr Hyssop looked sharply at her, as if he suspected her of trying to outwit him. 'Did your uncle tell you that? There are some stories that say the giant was originally meant to be a likeness of the Hunter. The same pious fools who built the church here must have erased his horn and spear and antlers, although they dared not do away with him entirely. But I am surprised your uncle knew of it.'

'He doesn't,' said Utterly. 'I saw them. With my own eyes. In the moonlight yesterday night. I looked out from my window and saw the giant had a horn in one hand and a spear in the other. And there were antlers on his head.'

'The child's been dreaming, I'll wager,' said Mr Inshaw. 'It is too much cheese before bed that does it.'

'So it would seem,' agreed Hyssop, but he was looking at Utterly with a strange, wondering light in his eyes. 'Or perhaps there is a whisper of Wildsea magic in Miss Dark. Perhaps her eyes detect some quality of moonlight that ours do not perceive. What do you see now, girl? Tell me.'

Utterly went to the window. Night had fallen while they talked. She put her face close to the pane and cupped her hands around it to cut out reflections. The moon had grown smaller and paler as it rose. It was riding now through wreaths of thin cloud high above the downs.

For a moment the chalk giant on his hill looked just as he had the first time Utterly saw him. Then, faintly, like the farthest stars swimming into vision when you have stared for a very long time at the night sky, the curved line of his horn and the straight upright shaft of his spear appeared, and from his head the wide nine-pointed antlers spread themselves like hoar frost over the down-land grass.

'There!' said Utterly.

'Where? What? I can't see anything,' said Mr Inshaw, coming to stand with her at the window. 'There is just the plain old giant on the hill, as he always has been.'

'I cannot see it either,' said Dr Hyssop. 'But Miss Dark can. Can't you, Utterly? You would not lie about such things, would you? Remember, your uncle's life depends on it.'

Utterly shook her head. 'It is no lie, sir. I see the horn and the spear only faintly, but they are there. He holds the horn in his left hand, and the spear in his right.'

'And does the spear have a blade to it, or is it just a line?'

Utterly lifted up her eyes to the hills again. 'There is a sort of pointy leaf-shape at the top of the spear, and it shines a little brighter than the rest.'

'Ha!' Dr Hyssop gave a short, sharp laugh of triumph. 'Perhaps we have been searching in the wrong place. What if the spear was never here among the stones at all, but up there, upon the down? Come, Inshaw. The game's afoot! I shall fetch my pick and spade. We must climb the giant's hill before the moon sets.'

'But, I say, Hyssop, what about young Utterly?'

'Oh, she will be coming with us. Miss Dark shall be our guide.'

Utterly supposed she had no choice in the matter. *At least it will keep Dr Hyssop busy*, she thought. *If he is climbing hills to search for magic spears he will not be tempted to go out shooting pistols at poor Egg again.*

Poor Egg. But even Dr Hyssop had said the boy might have escaped. Utterly prayed that it was so. As Mr Inshaw led her out of the Rectory and started along the path to the giant's hill she looked down towards the river, and the dark trees there, and hoped with all her heart that Egg was safe.

17

NIGHT BOAT TO WILDSEA

But Egg by that time was being washed swiftly down-river on the greatest flood the Swayle had ever seen. The sluicegate of the Grange's ornamental lake had mysteriously given way, and the lake's waters were rushing seawards. Egg rode them, clinging for dear life to the mossy timbers of the punt. By rights the wave should have ploughed the punt under or rushed on ahead of it and left it drifting, but the river girl had arranged somehow for it to balance on the wave's crest, and as it careered downstream she swam beside it, and ahead of it, and beneath it, and popped her head up sometimes out of the turmoil of the waters to shout with laughter at Egg's discomfort.

At the bend below Barrowchurch, a dead tree leaning out across the river almost brained him – he ducked just in time, and felt the bough whisk past above. At Bishop's Spivey, he was nearly hurled overboard when the punt struck jarringly against one of the piers of the bridge. 'Better pick up that punt pole,' jeered the river girl. 'Who knows what you'll slam into next if you're too lazy to fend off?'

Sometimes, when the Swayle was joined by smaller streams and tributaries, Egg noticed that the girl had turned into twins, or even triplets. Then she was just herself again, but bigger and stronger than before. By the time they reached Summertide Town she was a larger and older person entirely. The river had lost its enthusiasm for the game by then, and flowed as lazily as ever. The river woman gave the punt a last shove to carry it beneath the town's famous bridge, and called out, 'Here I'll leave you, boy. It's all salt sea from here, and tar, and fish-heads. Don't you forget to bring me back some cake.'

Egg turned to wave, but she was already gone; a swirl in the water above the bridge and then nothing, as if an otter had been swimming there. The night-time sky above the town was clear. He nursed his bruises, shivered inside his wet clothes, and waited impatiently for the punt to carry him up against one of the slimy posts beneath the wharves. It filled with water as Egg scrambled out, and had sunk by the time he reached dry land.

He stood in the moonlight, getting his bearings, sniffing the salt sea air, listening to drunken sailors roistering in the maze of streets behind the harbour.

'Lord bless and save us!' said Sal Varley, when he walked into the Mermaid tavern ten minutes later. 'I'd say you looked like a drowned rat if you were not so wet, and had a bit more meat on you! Well, don't just stand there dripping on my floor! Come through and sit you by the kitchen stove.'

'There ain't time,' said Egg. 'Is Captain Varley about?'

Captain Varley was about, but he was down at the docks with the *Whimbrel*, so there was time to eat a plate of boiled cod and cabbage before he could be fetched to the Mermaid. By the time he arrived Egg was starting on a second bowl, wrapped in a blanket while his clothes steamed in front of Sal Varley's range.

In Egg's mind, what should happen next was simple. He had planned it all out on his way downriver. He would explain what was going on at Barrowchurch, Captain Varley would believe him, and they would hurry aboard the *Whimbrel* and set sail for Wildsea to fetch Aish.

The first part went smoothly enough. Sal looked doubtful when he told them about the river girl and the haunted hill that had swallowed up Will Dark, but her brother was a sailor, and had heard of stranger things than that. His first instinct was to ride to Barrowchurch, but Egg convinced him that only Aish could deal with the magic of the place.

No, the trouble was the second part – the hurrying-aboard-the-*Whimbrel*-and-sailing-for-Wildsea part. For it

140

turned out the *Whimbrel* was not ready to go to sea, being halfway through loading stores and cargoes for a voyage to Falmouth. And the *Whimbrel*'s crew were even less seaworthy, for they had just been paid, and were spending their earnings in the taverns of the town. 'That's some of them now,' said Captain Varley, jerking his thumb in the direction of the Mermaid's public bar, where rowdy voices were more-or-less singing *The Coast of High Barbaree*. 'It's just you and me left sober, Egg my lad, and even if the dear old *Whimbrel* was shipshape, why, we couldn't steer her to Wildsea just the two of us. I'm happy to take you, but we can't leave afore tomorrow night.'

'What about Ted Beard's yawl?' asked his sister.

'Ay, Ted Beard's yawl might answer,' mused the captain.

'What's Ted Beard's yawl?' asked Egg.

'It's a little small boat that was left me in his will by a man named Ted Beard, in lieu of paying his bills,' Sal explained. 'Which I'd sooner of had the money, but she's a good yawl, and shallow enough in her draught to take you out even on this tide. I reckon Captain Varley could steer her to Wildsea easy enough, with the wind set fair and you to help him. I'm not sure I believe all you told us, Egg, but it's pretty clear *something* misfortunate has happened to poor Mr Dark, and if that's the case then his wife deserves to know of it.'

So it was decided, and long before dawn began to lighten the darkness that hung over Summertide, the yawl, with all her red sails set and Captain Varley at the tiller, was making her way out into the straits. Egg sat amidships, remembering the only other voyage he had made in a boat of that size, when he set out with Will Dark from Wildsea to seek the Hidden Lands. What they had found there or done there he could not recall, but they had gone to find Utterly, he remembered that, and they had found her too, and come home in triumph. So it had not really been a bit like this voyage, where he was sailing away from danger instead of towards it, and leaving Utterly behind.

He told himself that this was still the best plan he had. He told himself that Aish would know how to set everything right. But it still felt horribly as if he was running away.

18

A FISH OUT OF WATER

'People draw,' Aish had once told Utterly. They had been snuggled up together on the sofa at Sundown Watch at the time, leafing through a folio of little watercolour sketches that Will's late mother had made. 'Drawing is one of those things that makes people different from animals. I have known some clever crows, and some very wise dogs, but none of them would ever pick up a pencil or start carving on a stone. They let the world go by them, and are content to watch it pass. It is only people as feel the need to try and make it stand still by drawing pictures of it.'

Here in the Vale of Barrowchurch, lacking stones or paint or hot-pressed watercolour paper, the people of long ago had drawn their pictures on the land itself. But their drawing was made to be viewed from a distance; from the top of the Knoll, perhaps. The chalk giant looked very magnificent towering over Utterly as she made her way across the fields from the Rectory with Dr Hyssop and Mr Inshaw, but as they climbed up nearer to him he turned squat and foreshortened, until it became hard to tell he was a giant at all. By the time they reached his feet they had no sense of standing in the outline of a man any more; he was just various chalky paths leading away at different angles up the steep hillside.

'The villagers clear the lines of grass and moss each spring,' said Mr Inshaw. 'It's an ancient tradition, you see. Walking the giant's outline is meant to bring good luck.'

Utterly thought she could do with some good luck, plodding up the long outside line of the giant's right leg, not knowing where Egg had gone, not knowing what had become of Uncle Will, not even knowing if either of them was still alive. Dr Hyssop led the way, looking like nothing so much as a grave robber, with a lantern in one hand and a pickaxe over his shoulder. Mr Inshaw puffed along behind carrying the heavy spade.

With her captors so laden, Utterly wondered if it might be worth trying again to escape. The moon was bright, but the shadows were deep, and she felt sure she could find somewhere on the downs to hide. But what would that avail her? It would not help Egg, who was who-knew-where by now. Nor Uncle Will, lost in that wood beyond

144

the vanished stone door. Of the two of them, Utterly was more inclined to worry about Uncle Will. It was her duty to help Dr Hyssop find this spear, she decided, and hope he had told the truth when he said it would buy Will Dark's release.

They tramped up the giant's hip, then up his flank into the angle of his armpit. Utterly wondered if he could feel them there, like three fleas tickling him with their tiny feet. They turned a sharp corner and started along the inside of his arm. His hand, when they reached it, was a wide, wobbly oval of moonlit chalk with a rug of dark grass growing in the middle. Above it, and below, the line of the spear was a faint blue phosphorescence down in the roots of the grass, which only Utterly could see.

She stepped off the chalk and went uphill with Dr Hyssop and Mr Inshaw following. The blue light was strange. If Utterly looked down at it directly, it was hard to see at all, but if she looked ahead the shaft of the spear was quite clear, running up the steep scarp to a place level with the giant's head, where it divided into two lines, curving away from each other and then meeting in a point, marking out the leaf-shaped spearhead.

'We are here,' said Utterly, stepping into the centre of the leaf shape.

Dr Hyssop hastened up to join her, swinging his lantern to and fro, scanning the ground for signs of a chamber where something might lie buried. There was nothing; only the clover and the grass, and a few white moths blundering through it, disturbed by his lantern-light.

'If you are lying, girl,' he warned, down on his hands and knees now, feeling the indentations of the hill, 'if you have led us up here on a wild goose chase, with your talk of blue lights . . . Where is the point of the spearhead?'

'We are standing in it, but I can't see the light now,' said Utterly, dazzled by the lantern. She turned away, blinking. There was really no need for a lantern at all, she thought, not with the full moon riding in the starry sky above the downs, casting down such a bright, pale light. Abstract portions of the giant stretched away from her across the slope of the down; the curving pathways of his shoulder and the side of his head. Further down, in the darkness of his broad chest, another faint blue shimmer showed beneath the grass.

'There!' she said, pointing, forgetting that only she could see the light. 'Down there, where the giant's heart would be.'

'Show me!' said Dr Hyssop.

Utterly hurried across the hillside, stumbling in rabbit holes and startling up more of the pale moths. She reached the place where the blue light was. For a moment, as she looked down at it, she thought she could see through the grass and through the chalk beneath, as if it were water. A million tiny particles seemed to drift on the current there. Through them, dimly, she made out the shape of something box-like, not far below the surface.

'There are some stones,' she said, turning to call to Dr Hyssop and Mr Inshaw as they came blundering across the rabbit burrows behind her. 'Four stones, with a big flat one laid across the top.' She looked down again, but she could no longer see through the chalk. The blueness lingered like an after image. She stepped back, pointing to the place. 'It is here.'

'If you are lying . . .' said Dr Hyssop again, shining his lantern over the spot. It looked by lantern-light no different from any other portion of the down.

'It is buried,' said Utterly. 'But I don't think it is very deep.'

She sat down as the gentlemen started to dig. Mr Inshaw was clearly not used to such labours. He was soon to be heard complaining of backache and blisters, and kept stopping to wipe perspiration from his brow, or pick splinters of spade-handle from his hands. But Dr Hyssop never paused, just kept swinging the pick down, tugging it free of the shattered chalk, raising it high, swinging it down again, like a clockwork man.

'Stop your whining, Inshaw,' he growled. 'Splinters? What do a few splinters matter? We are drawing close to the source of all mysteries. The kind of power that has not been seen since the world was young and men cowered in terror before their wild gods. Why do you

147

think I pestered His Grace the bishop to make me vicar here? The stones, the Knoll, the giant, the legend of the stag . . . There is power in these hills of yours, Inshaw, though your people have always been too stupid to see it. Well, *I* see it, and if I can wake it, and win its favour . . .'

Utterly half listened, and thought about what she had seen, the way the chalk had seemed like moonlit water. A fox barked, way off across the valley somewhere. She watched the waves of wheat move through the fields below, and the wave-forms of the hills themselves rearing up dark against the sky. She lay back on the dew-damp grass and watched the stars. Slowly the chunk of the pick and the crunch of the spade lulled her to sleep, and she dreamed she was floating on a wide ocean, far from sight of land.

The boat that she had dreamed of once before swept past her, and the sea foamed white beneath its forefoot as the sailors adjusted their table-cloth sail to catch the wind. The boat curved in towards a marshy landing place between white cliffs, and Utterly in her dream went with it. She watched it pass the cluster of reed-roofed huts at the river's mouth, and move on upstream, sail down now, oars out, rowing through the shadow of deep-wooded hills. The river was the Swayle, much wider in the dream than it was in waking life. It carried the boat at last to a place she recognized as Barrowchurch, although that too was strangely changed, for all the river-meadows were mere marshes, and the hills were shaggy with scrub. There was another cluster of huts near where the Grange should stand. There the boat was tied up, and there the young man with the white band of mourning on his brow was set ashore. People came out of the huts to stare at him. He opened the bag he had brought with him and showed them the Hunter's carven horn. He unwrapped the long bundle he carried, and inside it was a spear.

When Utterly woke, her face and clothes and hair were damp with dew, and the sky was starting to grow pale. It was strange to wake with nothing above her but the fading stars and nothing beneath her but the hill. It took her a moment to remember how she came to be there. Then she heard a grunt, and the chink of the pick-axe, and looked round to find Dr Hyssop and Mr Inshaw still at work. They stood chest deep in the hole they had made, with the lantern burning on the grass beside it.

Utterly wondered if she had been forgotten. Far below her a winding line of mist curled through the Vale of Barrowchurch, hanging above the Swayle, and she wondered if Egg was hiding in it, safe under the river-side trees. Perhaps he was looking up right this instant, wondering why a lantern was shining on the chalk giant's breast.

As she crouched there, half inclined to flee, her gaze fell on the heap of broken chalk and flints that the digging had thrown up. One particular chunk of chalk caught her attention, though she was not sure why.

The gentlemen busy in their pit ignored her as she walked over to their spoil-heap and picked up the stone. It was not big or heavy, and it fitted satisfyingly into Utterly's cupped hand. A crack as black and fine as a single hair from her head ran down the whole length of it. Utterly fitted her thumbnails into the crack, and pulled. The stone opened like a book, and there inside . . .

'A fish!' she said, so loudly that Dr Hyssop and Mr Inshaw looked round at her. Mr Inshaw, glad of an excuse to stop digging, threw his spade aside and climbed out of the pit to take a drink from his hip flask. Then he came around the spoil-heap and looked down at what Utterly was holding.

Inside the stone, like a dried flower pressed between its chalky pages, was a fish. Or, at least, the bony, stony memory of a fish. The chalk glowed in the dim morning twilight, and the fish lay dark upon it; a lost minnow from some ancient sea.

'Oh! A stone-fish,' said Mr Inshaw, holding up the lantern so he might see it better. He was so covered in chalk dust, and so flecked with mud, he looked like one of those gentlemen from the last age who powdered their faces and hair, and stuck on beauty spots. 'My sister and

I used to go looking for stone-fish when we were young 'uns. Never caught one as fine as this, though. They are to be found all over the downs, you know. I suppose they were washed up here in the Flood, and turned to stone, poor creatures. The quarrymen dig them out of chalk pits sometimes. They are said to bring good luck . . .'

'If these hills are as full of good luck as you claim,' said Dr Hyssop, 'I am surprised you have not had more of it, Inshaw.' He had left the pit himself to see what was happening, and glanced without much interest at Utterly's find. He snatched Mr Inshaw's flask from him and took a long drink from it, then turned to his pit again, wiping his mouth on a grimy shirt-cuff. 'Come on, Inshaw; no idling. We are nearly there. Help me lever off the lid . . .'

Inshaw took back his flask, looked displeased at how little was left in it, and returned it to his pocket. He set down the lantern, and scrambled back down to join Dr Hyssop in the hole. Utterly stood looking at her fish. It was the best thing she had ever found, not just because it was so pretty and so perfect, but because it told her something about these hills she stood upon. *The sea was here once*, she thought. *Here where these waves of long grass blow and the ocean feels so far away, real waves once rolled, and real live fishes swam.* When she looked at the fish she could almost feel the salt breeze blowing on her face. It was as good as a glimpse of the sea itself.

'Steady there, Inshaw,' said Dr Hyssop. 'That's it – no,

get the spade under the brim there, you clodpoll! That's right – easy does it . . .'

Mrs Skraeveling, who sewed Utterly's frocks, always insisted on putting a pocket in the skirts. Lucy Dearlove said pockets for girls weren't genteel, but they were certainly useful, and Utterly was very glad of hers now. She wrapped the two halves of the stone very carefully in her handkerchief, put it in her pocket, and went to see what was happening in the pit.

Dr Hyssop and Mr Inshaw had been working hard while she slept. They had dug out a hole several feet in depth, and a yard or more across. In its bottom the thing she had glimpsed by moonlight lay exposed. It consisted of four upright stones, just as she had seen, with a larger slab laid across their tops, forming the lid of a crude stone chest.

This larger stone was what the gentlemen were struggling to remove. It was not chalk, but some harder substance, like the stones in the circle on the common, and it clearly weighed a lot. But they lifted it at last, and heaved it aside, and there beneath it was revealed a narrow chamber. Utterly was sure it looked too small to hold a spear, but Dr Hyssop gave a shout of triumph and, stooping, snatched up something that had lain there hidden for more centuries than Utterly could imagine. He seemed as delighted with it as she had been with her fish, and was so busy gloating over it that it was several moments before she or Mr Inshaw had a chance to see it for themselves.

'Is it treasure, Hyssop?' Mr Inshaw asked. 'Is it the Hunter's spear? Is there anything more? Any gold, perhaps? Or silver?'

'It is the spear alone,' said Hyssop, 'but the spear is all I need.'

'Speak for yourself,' grumbled Mr Inshaw. 'I should not have minded some gold and silver.'

'This is more valuable than a mountain of gold,' murmured Dr Hyssop, and held up his find so that the light of the early morning fell upon it. It was a blade as long as a man's forearm, with a socket at one end where it had once been fitted onto a wooden shaft. The metal was dark and dulled, but along the edges, where it narrowed to a point, the light lay hard, hinting at a deadly sharpness.

'Bronze?' said Mr Inshaw, holding the lantern near it. 'What on earth use is a *bronze* spear? It's too soft.'

'When every other blade in the world was made of stone, Inshaw, this was a thing of devastating power. And it still is. Look at how well it is preserved! It was made when the world was new, and the Hunter blended his own magic with the metals.' Dr Hyssop was turning the spearhead over and over in his hands as he spoke, rubbing it clean, tracing the wavering iridescent lines that wandered across the surface of the metal. 'I should have

153

guessed where it lay hidden,' he said. 'It is his strength. It is his heart.'

'Well, you have found it last, thanks to Miss Dark,' said Mr Inshaw. 'Now let us go to the Underwoods and give it back to this Hunter fellow, and free my sister and Cousin Will. But first I mean to walk Miss Dark home to the Grange. We have had the poor child up here all night. She must be hungry and thirsty, not to mention drenched by this beastly dew.'

Utterly felt grateful for his thoughtfulness. She *was* hungry, and she *was* thirsty, although she had not noticed either till Mr Inshaw mentioned them.

But Dr Hyssop said, 'Nonsense. We still have need of Miss Dark's services.'

'Do we, Hyssop? Why?'

'The door to the Underwoods is fickle, Inshaw. It does not open to just anyone. It may not open for me, even though I bear the Hunter's horn and spear. But it opened yesterday for Will Dark. Why? I could not fathom it – he is a perfectly commonplace young man. But then it came to me – he had Utterly with him. And Utterly has some power about her. Don't you, Utterly? Some connexion to the deep magics that govern the world, which modern men have grown too blind to see.'

He had climbed out of the pit and now stood over Utterly, looking down at her, fingering the sharp edge of the Hunter's spear. Utterly recalled a disagreeable moment on Wildsea when Thurza Froy the sea witch had tried to sacrifice her to summon up the Gorm. She hoped Dr Hyssop was not going to propose something of the same sort. She said, 'At Sundown Watch sometimes, the sea spoke to me. I have walked upon the shore of the Hidden Lands, and in the white gardens of the deep. The Gorm is . . .' She hesitated, frowning. The memories she needed most seemed always to hang just out of reach. But her hand, without her meaning it to, found its way into her pocket, and clutched the stone-fish, and the touch of it calmed her. 'The Gorm looks kindly on me, sir,' she said.

'The Gorm!' said Dr Hyssop. 'Of course!'

'The Gorm?' snorted Mr Inshaw. 'You don't mean to tell me the Gorm's real too? It's just an old story, ain't it?'

'A story with the power to send a tempest out of the western deeps that shook our islands to their roots and woke the Hunter in his secret woods,' said Dr Hyssop. His back was to the eastern sky and his face was in shadow, but Utterly knew he was watching her because the hard gleam of the spearhead was reflected in his eyes. 'The stone door did not open yesterday for Will Dark: it opened for this girl. Utterly is touched with the power of the Gorm, and the Gorm is as old and as powerful as the Hunter. We shall take Utterly to the door, and the door will open for her. Come on.'

He turned and strode swiftly away, tucking the spearhead into a deep inner pocket of his coat. 'Touched with the power of the Gorm?' grumbled Mr Inshaw, running a chalky hand through his chalky hair. 'Somebody is touched with something, that's for sure. Most unsuitable manners in a gentleman of the cloth. But we must do as he says, I suppose. Come, my dear; at least it is all downhill.'

He followed Dr Hyssop, and Utterly went with him, glad that he was there to protect her. As they reached the foot of the down and started through the fields to the Rectory she looked back and saw the giant again as he was meant to be seen, standing upon the steep hill's side to greet the dawn as the sun rose over the eastern downs. Where his heart should be, the scar of the night's diggings showed white. The lantern must still be burning there, she thought, for neither Mr Inshaw nor Dr Hyssop had thought to bring it with them. But the light of the new day was gathering so fast by then, she could not see the flame.

19

ANOTHER GREEN WORLD

They called in at the Rectory. Utterly went with Mr Inshaw to the pantry, where they ate stale bread with butter, and Utterly drank a mug of water. Dr Hyssop vanished into the depths of the house, where they could hear him banging and thumping.

'I still do not understand how Dr Hyssop can be so sure the Hunter will release Miss Inshaw and Uncle Will in return for his spear,' said Utterly.

'The Hunter said so,' said Mr Inshaw. 'He said he would release my sister, at least. We can only hope he will turn out to be a man of his word – or, well, a *thing* of his word.'

'But Dr Hyssop said the Hunter cannot leave the Underwoods,' said Utterly. 'And the door to the

Underwoods will not open for Dr Hyssop. So he cannot have spoken with the Hunter.'

'No, indeed,' said Mr Inshaw. Then, after a moment's awkward silence, he added, 'But you see, I have.'

He went to stand by the window with his back to Utterly, as if he were ashamed to face her. 'I do not remember it,' he said. 'That is the strange thing. You would think such a bizarre encounter would be burned indelibly upon my memory, but there is barely a trace. I remember going out to look for Elizabeth on the morning after the storm – a dreadful morning it was, the wind still wild, trees down everywhere, puddles in the lane, the river up over the footbridge . . . And then I was at home again. I think in the hour or so I lost I had dreamed of a stag, a black stag . . .'

'Magic is like that,' said Utterly. 'It sort of slides off your memory, like jelly sliding off a plate.'

'Really? You are so young, Miss Dark, yet you know so much more than I. Anyway, there I was, back at the Grange, with only my dream of a stag and the mud on my boots to show for my wanderings. And still no sign of Lizzie. So I set forth all over again, and this time when I reached the Knoll I found Hyssop there, poking around among the roots of the oak. "Back again, Inshaw?" says he, and I say, "What do you mean, 'again'?"

'And then Hyssop told me that I had been there just an hour before, when he had seen me come stumbling out of a doorway in the hill that closed up behind me. It seems I was carrying poor Lizzie's bonnet, and I had babbled at him about a forest I had found inside the Knoll, and how I had met a . . . a *person* there who told me I must fetch him his spear and horn and he would spare poor Lizzie and send her home.

'And when Hyssop told me, I found I did remember parts of it, so I was sure he was not lying, though the memories have faded again since. Dashed bad luck I call it – the only truly exciting or important thing that ever happened to me in my life, and I can't recall a single thing about it. All I remember is Hyssop telling me what I told him I had seen and heard. "Don't tell anyone else," he said, "or they shall say you have gone mad." And he concocted the tale of Lizzie being thunderstruck, and scorched the oak with gunpowder, and held Lizzie's bonnet in the flames – I had left it lying there, you see.

'You may imagine how guilty I felt, Miss Dark. And also how disturbed. For if I had endured this strange adventure but had no memory of it, then what else might I have done unknowingly? There was no way of knowing! That is why I felt I must break off my engagement to dear Jane Raftery. After all, a fellow can hardly ask a young lady to put her trust in him when he cannot even trust his own recollections . . .'

'But if the door to the Underwoods will open for you, why does he need me?' wondered Utterly.

'Oh, it has never happened since,' said Mr Inshaw miserably. 'I lose count of the times Hyssop has had me stand beneath that wretched oak with him, shouting "abracadabra" and "open sesame" and calling on heathen gods whose names he finds in those foul old books of his, but the door remains shut. It is as if I have lost the knack. Or perhaps I never had it, and it was only because of the storm that night the door stayed open for a while. Dr Hyssop says . . .'

He broke off, for Dr Hyssop himself could be heard outside the room. When he opened the door and came in they saw that he had fitted the spearhead onto a long shaft of ash-wood. He carried the Hunter's horn, too, hanging from a cord around his neck.

'It is time,' he said.

He led them out through the back of the house and up the steep, crooked steps to the church. Mist drifted between the trees, making the old oak look more huge and haunted than ever as they crossed the church-yard and went down through the lych gate. They left the path and stepped across the oak's roots to the place where the stone door had been.

'Open the door,' said Dr Hyssop.

'I do not know how,' retorted Utterly. 'It is not the sort of door that opens if you simply knock, or tug upon a bell-rope. It was already open when I came here yesterday, and then it closed, and I could not open it again.' But she thought of Uncle Will, lost and in need of her, and she went and placed her hand upon the roots, roughly where she had last seen him standing. And suddenly, although she did not see the change occur, the roots were gone; the door was there; and the light of another, greener world was spilling out on her.

'Great Heavens!' shouted Mr Inshaw, stumbling backwards in his surprise. He tripped on a tree root and sat down heavily. 'Ow!'

The sunlight streaming through the doorway felt warm upon Utterly's face, and once again she could hear that sound; the soft sigh and rush of the sea on a gentle shore. But once again, before she could step through the doorway, she was pulled aside. It was Dr Hyssop this time, and he dragged her out of his way quite roughly as he strode past her to the door. He turned on the threshold, pointed the Hunter's spear at Utterly, and said, 'Inshaw, take her back to the Rectory; await me there.'

'But what of Elizabeth?' asked Mr Inshaw feebly. 'I must come with you and save her . . .'

'Only he who rules the Underwoods can save her,' snapped Dr Hyssop. 'And you would be struck dumb at the very sight of him and then rush out babbling, as you did once before. You are of no further use to me, you quivering milk pudding.'

'Now, I say, Hyssop, that's a bit strong . . .'

'I shall go alone to pay my homage, and beg the

Hunter to release your fellow milk pudding of a sister, if he has not already eaten her. You will take Miss Dark to the Rectory.'

He turned, stooped under the lintel, and was gone. Mr Inshaw struggled to his feet and brushed leaf mould and beech mast off his breeches. Utterly looked at the shining door again. How long would it wait? She was scared to go into it, but she was scared not to, in case it disappeared again. *Uncle Will must have been scared too*, she thought. *When he set out for the Hidden Lands to fetch me home, he must have been just as scared as I am now, but he set out anyway . . .*

'Come then, Miss Dark,' said Mr Inshaw. 'We'd best do as Hyssop says. He's doubtless right – he usually is – though I wish he weren't so confounded rude about it.'

But Utterly had made up her mind. Uncle Will needed her. She could not trust Dr Hyssop to save him. She reached in her pocket, pulled out her stone, and unwrapped it. When she opened it she saw that the half that did not have the fish in still held its imprint; a perfect negative of a fish, like a jelly-mould. Without thinking, but knowing somehow it was important, she nestled that half down among the roots. Then she put the half with the fish back into her pocket, and ran to the stone door.

'Miss Dark!' shouted Mr Inshaw, but Utterly was already inside the Knoll, and his voice seemed to come from far, far away. She pushed her way along a narrow passage between big slabs of stone, and stepped into the Underwoods.

❖

Trees surrounded her, impossibly huge and old. The sound she had taken for the sound of the sea was just the wind of that other world, pouring through the immense canopies of leaves above her head. In this world there were only trees, and Utterly felt even further from the sea than she had at Barrowchurch.

She could not hear Dr Hyssop, or see any sign of which way he had gone with the horn and spear. Various paths led away through the undergrowth, all looking aimless and untrustworthy, as if they had been made by animals. It would be horribly easy to get lost here, Utterly thought. Paths would move around. North and south, east and west, would not stay where you left them, and nothing would stay for long in your memory. But she reached in her pocket and ran her thumb over the stony fossil of the fish, and found that it reminded her very clearly of the world outside, where the other half of her stone lay waiting to be reunited with the half she held. When she left it there she had not fully realized what she was doing, it had simply seemed the right thing to do. Now she understood that, for as long as she had the fish, she would remember her way back to the stone door. It was like that thread which the Greek gentleman in the story had used to find his way through the Labyrinth.

She walked a little distance along the nearest path and called, 'Uncle Will! Uncle Will!'

There was no answer. The trees held their silence. They were dreaming their long dreams, and Utterly had the uneasy feeling that if she shouted too loudly she might awaken them. They formed a kind of living labyrinth, she thought, and somewhere amongst them lurked something far worse than any Minotaur.

'Uncle Will!'

She heard a sound. A voice, she thought. Had it been Uncle Will's? She could not tell, it was so faint. But when she called his name again she thought she heard it answer, 'Here!'

The sound had come from somewhere to her right, where the ground sloped steeply downhill and a rickety stairway of roots descended between the pillars of the trees. Utterly clambered down them. Between the roots was dark loam that she sank knee-deep in. As she went down, the trees grew more dense, and the shadows deepened. Mushrooms and toadstools grew everywhere, some singly, some clustering in crowds. Some were red with white spots; some were tiny, delicate things that seemed made of bone-china; some were great fleshy trumpets, some had caps like rotted peaches, or old poppy petals, or fresh-baked scones, or tiny porcelain cups of purple ink.

164

Puffballs burst beneath Utterly's boots and let out their grey mist of spores like pent-up breaths. Dryad's saddles and wood-chicken jutted from the trunks of the trees, and earth-stars gazed up at her like leathery little eyes from the places between their roots.

The musty scent of all those fungi hung heavily in the air as Utterly came to the bottom of the slope. The dark soil was even deeper here; formed by layers of leaves that had fallen and rotted for a thousand autumns with nothing to disturb them, only the earthworms and insects burrowing through their darkness. If Utterly listened closely, she could hear things scuffling and slithering around down there. When she scuffed the top layer of the leaf-mould aside, the under-layers were webbed with fine white traceries of mould.

'Uncle Will!' she called.

'Here, child,' came the answer.

The voice seemed to come from beneath the leaf-mould. It was not Uncle Will's.

A few yards away a ring of toadstools glowed wetly white against the black soil. The smallest were no bigger than Utterly's fist, but the largest were as broad as dinner-plates. As she watched, a new one pushed its way up through the skeleton leaves that lay like lace upon the surface. Corpse-white like the rest, but soon far larger, it shouldered its neighbours aside. As it rose, its domed top spread out into a parasol three feet across, perched like

165

a broad-brimmed hat upon a slender white stalk twice as tall as Utterly.

In the shadows beneath the hat, two jet-black eyes opened, and regarded Utterly beadily. A lipless mouth curved upward at each end, like a drawing of a smile. 'Human child!' it said. 'Oh, welcome! Welcome!'

Slender arms split from the toadstool's stalk with soft tearing sounds. Delicate white hands reached out to Utterly, beckoning her forward into the waiting ring.

'I am looking for my uncle, ma'am,' said Utterly, staying where she was. 'He is lost in these woods somewhere, but I cannot find him.'

The toadstool tilted her wide parasol-hat on one side, and a gentle blizzard of spores snowed down from between its gills. The black eyes blinked. 'Poor child,' she said. 'These woods are very big, and my empire extends through every part of them. I have my outposts in the south-country where great armoured lizards lie dozing in warm pools, and in the north, where the trees are all hard green needles and the wolves howl all night long. Deeper than the deepest roots my pale children delve, and my lookouts keep their garrisons on the heights of the highest branches. But I have heard nothing of any lost uncles wandering in my domains. I expect he has died. All things do, you know; even the wolves, even the lizards in their coats of mail. They die, and sink down into the ground where I am waiting for them.

Come, dearest; come join me. We will search for your uncle together.'

Utterly shook her head. 'Dr Hyssop said it was the Hunter who ruled these woods.'

'The Hunter rules the world above-ground, but don't let that deceive you. All that lies below is mine, and all things come below eventually, down to bloom and moulder in the lovely dark.'

Again the pale hands beckoned. The toadstool queen's face still smiled, but it was freckled now with small black flies, which had been lured by her stench.

'Come, child,' she whispered. 'I shall show you the great webs I have spread through the darkness. Lie down in the soft ground, as all things must at last. Rest.'

'Child!' called another voice, from somewhere behind Utterly, and above. She glanced back. She could see nothing but the twilit trees standing sentinel behind her on the slope. Who had spoken? Had another of the talkative toadstools sprouted there?

'Pay no attention,' said the toadstool queen. 'You are mine. Come with me, and take your place in my empire of decay.'

As she spoke, she reached out her arms, which stretched much further than Utterly had expected, and her dusty white fingers caught hold of Utterly's hands. But she drew them back at once, as if the touch of Utterly's skin had burned her. 'No!' she cried. 'Oh no! Oh, *you* do not belong here! *You* are not of the land. Why would you try to trick me so, disguising yourself as a human child? I am of the land and the darkness under it, I make no claim upon the Gorm's realm. Go back!'

Utterly wanted to say, I am not disguised, I *am* a human child. But in her mind, a memory was rising like a vast wave, ready to break.

'Child!' came the voice from behind her again. The wave subsided without breaking. This time when Utterly looked behind her she clearly saw someone scrambling downhill between the trees, signalling frantically to her and calling out, 'Come away! Come away! Do not trust the White Queen!'

'Go back to your own deeps, Sea's Daughter!' said the toadstool woman angrily.

Utterly turned to her again, and saw that a change had come upon her. The parasol-hat was collapsing in slime and slithering down to hide her face; the white stalk of her body was weeping and wilting. A moment more and she was just a big toadstool, rather past its best. But from somewhere in the earth below, her voice still whispered, 'Sea's Daughter, go!'

'Why do you call me Sea's Daughter?' wondered Utterly.

'Oh, child!' said the other voice, and a warm, rough, reassuringly human hand caught Utterly's and pulled her backwards up the slope, away from the ring of toadstools.

'Oh, my dear, you are fortunate indeed that we found you when we did. This dell is one of the White Queen's pleasure grounds, and best avoided. Thank Heaven you are safe!'

Utterly's rescuer was a woman, quite short and rather thin, wearing a very tattered grey dress, and carrying a stick, which had been turned into a sort of spear by means of burning one end of it in a fire. It was impossible to make out her face, for she had a great deal of matted hair, and her head was turned away from Utterly as she led the way uphill through the trees. Another shape went bounding ahead of her; a shaggy, loping thing that Utterly could not quite put a name to, until it stopped to bark furiously at the toadstools in the dell behind them and the woman said, 'Quiet, Fig! Good dog! Brave dog! Be quiet!'

So it is a dog, thought Utterly, although she was still not quite certain.

They reached the top of the slope. The dog sniffed the air cautiously, then flung itself down upon the ground, while the woman propped her spear against a tree and set to tying her hair back with a strip of cloth. Then Utterly saw her clearly for the first time, and recognized her large nose and small chin. She was much more like her brother than the portrait in the Grange had made her seem.

'Oh, Miss Inshaw!' said Utterly. 'I am so pleased to find you well!'

20

THE CASTAWAY

Elizabeth Inshaw seemed surprised at being recognized. 'My word!' she said, coming closer and speaking very softly. 'But who are you, child? I thought you were some lost woodling, but by your clothes and your voice . . . Have you come from . . . that place whose name I have almost forgot . . . ?'

'I came from Barrowchurch,' said Utterly. 'My name is Utterly Dark and I was with your brother, Mr Francis Inshaw, not five minutes ago, outside the stone door.'

'Barrowchurch,' said Miss Inshaw. 'The stone door . . . Yes, I remember it . . .'

'Mr Inshaw has been very worried about you,' Utterly explained. 'He thinks you are being held a captive by a gentleman called the Hunter . . .'

'Shhh!' hissed Miss Inshaw, highly alarmed. 'Do not speak his name! He is hunting far off in the north, but I firmly believe he may hear you if you speak his name aloud, however far away he be. Even *thinking* it can call him, I fear. It is only thanks to God's mercy and this brave and helpful dog that I have managed to avoid falling into his hands.'

The dog in the shadows behind her shook itself, as if it were pleased to be mentioned. It would have wagged its tail, thought Utterly, but it did not seem to *have* a tail, poor thing.

'If you stay with us, dear girl, you may be spared too,' said Miss Inshaw.

'Thank you,' said Utterly. 'But I am going to find my way out, and you should come with me, Miss Inshaw.'

'Oh, poor child, there is no way out of the forest! It stretches on for ever and for ever. I have been here for – oh, I do not know how long, for there are no days and nights here. I have sought and sought for the passage that will lead me back home, and I have never yet been able to find it.'

'But I can,' said Utterly. She took out her stone fish. 'This fish used to swim in the hills of Barrowchurch when the hills were sea. I have left the other half of the stone, with its impression in, outside the door, and it is as if the two halves are joined by an invisible string. All we need do is follow it.'

Miss Inshaw came close and reached out to touch the fossil. 'Can this be true, child? I have been here so long, I scarcely dare to hope . . .'

'It is true,' said Utterly. 'But I cannot leave without I find my uncle first. Have you seen him? His name is Will Dark.'

'Oh dear,' said Miss Inshaw, looking from the fossil to Utterly's face. 'Oh, my poor child, I am so sorry. Your uncle is a handsome young man, quite tall, with dark hair?'

'Well, he is tall, and his hair is dark,' said Utterly. She had never thought of Uncle Will as handsome, but she supposed to someone who had been lost in an enchanted wood for months and months he might seem quite presentable. 'You have seen him then?'

Miss Inshaw nodded, but she looked upon the brink of tears. 'Then I have the most dreadful news. Perhaps you should sit down upon this fallen log. Your uncle was here a while ago. I tried to warn him, but he was afraid of me, and fled. It was not his fault, poor gentleman. *He* was prowling that night, and when *he* is on the prowl it is hard to think straight, or keep a grip upon one's reason at all. *He* has a way of driving all thoughts out of one's head. Your uncle fled from me, and . . . well, my dear, I am sorry to have to tell you that in his confusion he blundered into one of *his* traps.'

'Whose traps? The Hunter's?'

'Shhhh!'

Utterly had not sat down when Miss Inshaw suggested it, but now she wished she had. She felt as if the ground beneath her feet had suddenly turned to the thinnest ice, and was starting to crack, with a terrible dark abyss waiting beneath it. Tears came to her eyes. 'Are you saying, Miss Inshaw, that Uncle Will is . . . that he has been . . . Oh, please, Miss Inshaw, do not tell me that . . .'

'He has been taken to the Hunter's holt,' said Miss Inshaw, saying most of those words in a whisper and the name of the Hunter so quietly that it was barely a sound at all. 'The Hunter does that sometimes. When he catches pigs and deer and other beasts he kills them cleanly and butchers them straight away, but when he catches prey that has the power of thought, like one of the poor woodlings, he will sometimes take them to his holt, and keep them there in a wicker cage, as you or I might keep a songbird. He thrives on fear, you see, and the fear and sufferings of those poor souls as they slowly perish are as pretty as the songs of birds to him. It will be your uncle's suffering that is singing to him now. I am afraid there is no hope for the poor gentleman.'

'But if Uncle Will is alive,' said Utterly, drying her tears, 'then I must rescue him.'

'Oh, child, it would be madness to venture into *his* stronghold.'

173

'But the H . . . *he* is far away, hunting in the north, you said.'

'He may return. He moves swiftly.'

'Then I will move more swiftly,' declared Utterly. 'I cannot leave poor Uncle Will stuck in a cage. Where is this holt place?'

'It is in the gorge where the river begins.'

'Will you show me?'

Miss Inshaw looked so terribly afraid that Utterly felt cruel for having asked, but the shaggy dog-thing made a friendly sort of growling sound and nudged against Miss Inshaw's leg, and she looked down and patted its head and said, 'You are right, Fig; she is a *very* brave girl, and we must learn by her good example. Very well, Utterly Dark; we shall lead you to the holt. But if *he* has returned from his hunting, we must not go near. For however brave we are, we cannot hope to fight against *him*.'

Ten months in the Underwoods had changed Miss Inshaw so much that Utterly found it hard to remember this was the same lady who had written that whimsical fairy diary. She had grown into as hardened a castaway as Robinson Crusoe. She had taught herself to make the spears and snares she needed to catch food, as well as doeskin shoes to replace her worn-out slippers, and an eccentric birch-bark bonnet to keep off the rain. She could thread her way through the winding pathways of the forest as confidently as the animals that had made them. Trees that all looked much alike to Utterly were distinctive landmarks to Miss Inshaw.

She had wandered far in all directions from her little camp, and as she led Utterly towards the Hunter's holt she told her, in whispers, about some of the things she had seen. Go far enough north, she said, and there was frost on the ground, and snow in the air, and the trees turned to pines and larches. Once she had found a ruined house made out of stale and mouldering gingerbread. Once she had seen a huge, shaggy creature like a hairy elephant go barging its way through a stand of birches. Once she had discovered a place where bones and rusted armour lay scattered among the tree roots beside a dark pool, as if a dreadful battle had been fought there long ago. Several times she had caught fleeting glimpses of the people she called woodlings, frail-looking little folk who did not live in houses or huts or even tents, but wandered the forest in small bands, making nests for themselves in the crooks of trees, and never staying in one place for long. They were as frightened of Miss Inshaw as they were of the Hunter himself, so she had never found an opportunity to speak with them.

'I declare, I should have gone quite mad with loneliness,' she said, 'if it had not been for dear Fig.'

The shaggy dog-like thing led the way, bounding along the maze of paths and stopping sometimes to wait while Utterly and Miss Inshaw caught up. On those occasions it would sometimes give a soft, encouraging woof, almost as if it were talking to them.

'What type of dog is Fig?' asked Utterly.

'I am afraid I do not know his pedigree,' said Miss Inshaw. 'I confess, I do not even know where he came from. The night I arrived here I was so scared, for *he* was about, and the smell of *him* was on the air. I ran and ran, and fell down in a swoon, and when I woke, this noble creature was sitting by my side as if to guard me. We have been together ever since, and we have looked after one another pretty well, I think. Fig catches rabbits sometimes, and I make a little fire to cook them when I dare.'

'*Woof, gruff, woof,*' said Fig, pronouncing each sound very clearly.

'I am not entirely sure he *is* a dog, Miss Inshaw,' said Utterly. 'Perhaps he is a type of ape?'

The path sloped downward between wooded crags into a steep-sided valley of the sort that Wildsea people called a cleave. Green moss covered the rocks and trees, growing thicker and greener as the travellers descended. A river spoke softly, far below, rushing over stones. The trees stretched up their huge shaggy arms, and thick ropes of ivy twined about their trunks. Old trees had died and fallen and new trees had sprouted from their decay, and the White Queen's empire had raised toadstool colonies among the rot of them, and bred bracket fungi from dead trunks that still stood upright. The air smelled of life and death and the dark wet earth.

They crossed a stream, and stopped to drink from it. 'Not far now,' said Fig. Utterly was so lost in the green dream of the place, it took her a few seconds to realize he had spoken in English.

'Oh! He is not a dog or an ape at all!' she said, looking at him afresh. 'He is a man!'

As soon as she had said it, she could see that she was right. The shaggy creature was a small, wiry man, and not even really so very shaggy, except that his hair was rather long and his beard rather raggedy, and his corduroy breeches and old pink coat had been as badly tattered by the thorns as had Miss Inshaw's dress.

'Good Heavens!' said Miss Inshaw. 'You are right! Oh, my dear sir, I do apologize! I have been labouring under the impression you were a dog.'

Fig scratched his head thoughtfully and said, in a voice that started as a sort of growl and grew less dog-like with each word, 'That's all right, I'm sure, mistress. To be honest, I sort of thought I was a dog myself. There is something about this place that brings out the animal in people – oh, not in you mistress, no one could mistake you for nothing but a lady. But I was not much better

177

than a dog when I blundered in here, and so a dog is what I took to thinking I must be. And it was not so bad, to tell you the truth. Indeed, I think I was happier as a dog than I had been as a man. Things are so nice and simple when you are a dog: food is for eating, noises is for barking at, monsters is for scaring off, and the mistress is for protecting.' He glanced shyly towards Miss Inshaw, but seemed too bashful to meet her eye. 'It was a nice, straightforward sort of life.'

'But what is your name?' asked Utterly. 'It can't just be Fig. Can it?'

'Figgy Dan was what they called me, miss,' said the man. 'I think once I was called Daniel Figgis, but Figgy Dan is how I'm known now.'

'Oh!' cried Miss Inshaw. 'You came to the house once, when dear Papa was alive. He told us to make sure you were fed, because you had worn the king's uniform.'

'I wear it still, miss, though it is sadly faded,' said Figgy, plucking at his tunic sleeve. 'Yes, I remember it now. It was just as you say. Your father was a proper gentleman, miss, and most considerate.'

'But how did you come into the Underwoods?' wondered Utterly.

'I am not at all sure, miss. My memory has always been a bit untoward, you might say, ever since them guns got inside my head. I don't rightly remember how I come to be here.'

'Oh, but I do!' said Miss Inshaw. 'It all comes back to me! It was on the night of the storm, when I walked out to Barrowchurch Knoll and thought I had found the door into Fairyland. Fig – I mean, Mr Figgis – found me there, standing before the open portal. He warned me not to go inside, but I was such a silly creature in those days, and I would insist. So, with great gallantry, Mr Figgis came in after me. And somehow, in the confusion of finding ourselves in this forest, I came to think he was a dog.'

'I am loyal as any dog, I hope,' said Figgy Dan. 'And I have a good nose, and good sharp ears, for I can't hear no guns a-rumbling and a-booming all the time in here, which was a sore impediment to my hearing in the other world. And now my nose and my ears both tell me we are near *his* holt, and we should press on quick if we hope to help your poor uncle, Miss Utterly, before *he* returns.'

'Good dog,' said Miss Inshaw, from force of habit, and then, 'What I mean to say is, a capital idea, Mr Figgis.'

They went on down the path. Some of the trees they were passing now had horns and eye-sockets, or seemed to. Then Utterly realized that the skulls of animals had been tied to them and the moss had grown so thickly over the skulls that they appeared to be part of the trees.

Not all the skulls had belonged to animals.

The green light deepened. Trees grew out horizontally from the mossy cliffs. The river grumbled. There was a sudden sweetish smell of woodsmoke. Figgy Dan

179

stopped, crouching behind a fallen tree, and beckoned Utterly to come and see.

Ahead, the cleave narrowed to a dark cliff, and the river came out of a cleft in that cliff and flowed away through the forest. There was a wide cave at the cliff's foot, and in its mouth a fire smouldered: grey wood-ash and red embers in a stone-lined pit. The bones of butchered carcasses were scattered around the fire, and hundreds of animal and human skulls gazed down eyelessly from the surrounding trees.

'There,' said Figgy Dan. 'That is his holt. It is his age-old castle.'

Utterly supposed he must be joking, but he did not *look* as if he were joking. And when she looked at the cave again she could dimly see it as Figgy Dan must; not a cave at all, but an arched doorway carved into the living rock, with a glimpse of other doorways and pillared stairs within it, and narrow watchful windows piercing the cliff above, and a hint of battlements way up there where cliffs and trees and twilit sky blurred into one.

'Now you have seen *his* stronghold,' said Miss Inshaw, 'I am sure you will agree it is far too dangerous to venture in. We should not have brought you here. We should leave at once. *He* may return at any moment . . .'

'With the river so loud we may not hear *him* coming till *he* is right on top of us,' said Figgy Dan. 'We need a proper plan of attack, is what we need.'

But Utterly had no time for plans. Uncle Will had saved her from the Hidden Lands, and now she would save him from the Underwoods. She ducked under the fallen tree and ran to the cave mouth, ignoring the urgent whispers from Miss Inshaw and Figgy Dan telling her to come back.

21

A STRANGE AND
TERRIBLE KNOWLEDGE

The cave mouth was full of smoke from the fire, which looked as if had been burning there forever. Utterly closed her eyes as she walked through the thickest part of the smoke, and when she opened them again she was inside the cave. Once again, she glimpsed it as Figgy Dan must; high vaulted ceilings with stone columns to hold them up, and a wide stairway rising. But she could tell that was only a sort of mirage, and that really it was just a cave she stood in, with a passage opening off at the back of it. In the cave's centre stood a slab of stone, which seemed to serve the Hunter as a table and a butcher's block; it was caked with dried blood, and hunks of bloody meat lay on it, along with the flint knives that had been used to carve them.

Utterly checked that no one was about, then edged around the slab and hurried towards the passage at the rear. How was it that she could she see through the illusion of the place, and Miss Inshaw and Figgy Dan could not? As she ran up sloping shelves of rock that wanted her to believe they were stairs, she suddenly recalled the Hidden Lands, and how tricksy they had been; palaces that became sea-caves; beautiful brooches that turned out only to be starfish. Perhaps having been once in a place like that gave you an eye for magic, so you were not fooled next time you met it. 'And the Gorm is more powerful than this Hunter,' said Utterly to herself, 'for her ocean is older and more terrible than any forest, or any hunter. She was there at the very beginning of things, even before the Spirit of God moved on the face of the waters. So if I saw through her glamours I am hardly likely to be taken in by his . . .'

And again, just for a moment, she sensed that wave rear up inside her like a strange and terrible knowledge she was almost on the brink of understanding, and this time it almost broke over her. But then she recalled her desperate situation, and the wave subsided again, and she crept on.

The steep tunnel led her up into another cavern, almost as massive as the one below. It had smelly tallow lamps burning in crannies in the walls, and a pool in the middle of the floor. A pile of skins kept Utterly frozen to the spot for half a minute until she had wholly convinced herself that it was not a sleeping bear. The pool was mirror-like, and held the reflection of a cluster of cages hanging from the cave roof. The cages were woven from thick stems of ash or willow. In some of them Utterly saw white bones. In one, over at the far side of the cavern, a huddled shape stirred and groaned, and a hand gripped the wooden bars.

'Uncle Will?' Utterly whispered, and the walls and roof all whispered, 'Uncle Will! Uncle Will!'

The cage trembled and swung as the prisoner within twisted round to see her. 'Utterly?'

She ran around the pool and stood below him. His cage hung just above her head, and by standing on tiptoe she was able to reach up and clasp the hand he stretched down through the bars. 'What are you doing in this awful place, Utterly? How did you come here? No, it does not matter – you must leave at once! He has gone hunting, I think, but he will soon return, and he must not find you here!'

'That is just exactly what Miss Inshaw said,' said Utterly. 'We will leave together, Uncle Will.' She tugged at the cage, but it was well made, lashed together with tough lengths of hide. Spells had been woven into the knots so that it made Utterly's fingers tingle just to touch them.

'Wait,' she said, and ran back around the mirror pool

and down the tunnel to the lower cave, where those flint knives were lying on the Hunter's table.

They were big, dark flints, shining like blue-black glass in the fire-glow, chipped and knapped to wicked edges. Most were too big and heavy for Utterly's hands, but she found a smaller one, and took one of the big ones too, thinking Uncle Will could use it.

She was just about to run back up to him when something made her pause. Was that a sound from beyond the cave mouth? A heavy footfall, the clattering of dislodged stones in the entrance . . .

She looked up, just in time to see the Hunter loom out of the smoke.

At first she thought he was a black stag. His antlers came through the drifting smoke before the rest of him, and they were so wide, and so high up, and cast such strange shadows across the cave walls that she did not believe they could be attached to a human head. But human he was, more or less. The curtains of the smoke drew aside, and there he stood, immensely tall, immensely broad, wide-shouldered and barrel-chested, yet grey and shambling, as if a weight of many years was on him. His mane of grizzled hair hung down over his shoulders, and his beard tangled with the shaggy hair upon his body. His hands had horny talons, and were red with the blood of the boar he carried slung upon his back. His feet were the cloven hooves of a stag.

And he had smelled something. He dumped the carcass on the cave floor and lifted his head to sniff the air. Utterly imagined him thinking 'Fee-Fi-Fo-Fum', like the ogre in the tale of Brave Jack and his Magic Beanstalk. *He cannot possibly smell me,* she promised herself, crouching behind the slab-like table and praying he would not glance down at her. *I walked through all that smoke when first I came in, so I must smell of nothing but smoke . . .*

But the Hunter knew that some strange scent was in his holt. He turned, still sniffing for it, and the firelight fell upon his face. He looked too fierce and wild to be a person, but too human-like to be an animal. His eyes were golden, and their black pupils were up-and-down slits. He was entirely terrifying, just as Miss Inshaw and Figgy Dan had warned.

Utterly cowered from him behind the slab of stone, but there was not really enough room behind it to hide in, even for a girl who was small for her age. As the Hunter took one step and then another into the cave, Utterly knew he must soon look down and see her . . .

'Hunter!' shouted a new voice, from outside

The Hunter swung around. His antlers ripped raggedy holes in the smoke. Peeping from her hiding place, Utterly saw Dr Hyssop standing outside the cave mouth.

The Hunter made a soft growling sound deep in his chest. The hair on his back was bristling like the hackles of an angry dog.

'Great Hunter!' called Dr Hyssop in a pulpit voice, holding aloft the spear he carried. 'I have come from afar, and wandered a long while in your maze of trees. Hyssop is my name. I am here to return these things that were stolen from you.'

The Hunter straightened up at the sight of the spear, like an old soldier drawing himself to attention when a military band goes by. It made him even taller. He had forgotten the scent of Utterly; all his attention was fixed now upon Dr Hyssop. He took a step towards the cave mouth, and then another. Utterly saw her chance and fled, clutching a flint knife in either hand and running as fast and light-footed as ever she could to the stairs and up them.

'Utterly!' called Uncle Will, when she reached the inner cavern. She shushed him, desperately afraid the Hunter must have heard. But no stag-headed shadow came up the stairway behind her. (And it *was* a stairway now, she realized, as she crouched at the top of it, looking back. As if the Hunter's homecoming had strengthened the illusions of the place.)

Outside, Dr Hyssop said loudly, 'But stay, Hunter! There is a price to pay. One favour in return for another. You promised the man Inshaw he would have his sister back. But Inshaw is not here, and I am, and I say keep the lady if you wish. What I beg is a far lesser and far greater gift. I have done you this service, finding the horn and

187

spear, and bringing them into your woods. All I ask is that you allow me to go on serving you . . .'

How could he talk to the Hunter like that, thought Utterly. How did he not just fall down on his face and grovel? But there was no time for wondering. She scampered to Uncle Will's cage and pressed the larger of the flint blades into his hand. Then she began hacking away at the knots that held the cage together from below, while Uncle Will attacked them from above. 'Good girl!' he whispered as he worked. 'I have been dangling here I do not know how long, watching that monster gnaw on bones and fearing he would soon gnaw on mine. Now, let us consider this scientifically, Utterly; we need not cut the whole cage apart, we have only to make a small gap, just large enough to . . .'

At which moment the floor of the cage gave way, and he landed with an 'Oof!' and a splash in the pool, which was a shallow one, luckily. He scrambled up at once, wincing at the stiffness in his limbs, and let Utterly lead him back down the stairs.

They stopped when they reached the bottom, and peered cautiously through the smoke. The Hunter was outside the cave mouth now. He was standing in the twilight by the river, listening to Dr Hyssop.

'Hear me out, great Hunter!' the vicar was saying, as if he sensed that the Hunter was growing impatient. 'It is long years since you walked in the world of men. They have made many changes there while you kept to your own woods. They have cut down your forests, paved your heaths, covered your hills with teeming cities and proud towers, with smoky mills and manufactories . . .'

'What is Hyssop doing here?' hissed Uncle Will.

'He is serving himself, like the low deceitful villain he is,' Utterly whispered back. 'But while he has the Hunter distracted, we can run away.'

They edged through the bone-littered hall towards the door. There in the shadows they paused, trying to steel themselves for the dreadful flight across the stretch of open ground outside the holt to the place where the trees grew thickly, where Utterly hoped Miss Inshaw and Figgy Dan were still waiting. It was a distance of only twenty feet or so, but it might as well have been a hundred miles. There seemed no way that the Hunter, with his sharp nose and ears and watchful golden eyes, would not smell or hear or see them as they dashed past behind him. And even if, by some miracle, he did not, well, Dr Hyssop would see them, and betray them.

'Let me ride at your heels when you return to the world above, O King,' said Dr Hyssop. 'I will advise you about the new things you will meet there. With my help, your realm will spread once more across all the lands, and men shall worship you again, yes, even as you hunt them to their doom.'

The Hunter let out a long growl. It was hard to tell if he was agreeing with Dr Hyssop or not.

'Take back your spear, Great Hunter!' commanded Hyssop, and went down on one knee, holding out the spear. 'Take your spear, and your horn, and the fealty of your humble servant, Lemuel Hyssop!'

But the Hunter had never had any patience for human beings and their ways. What was this little whimpering creature asking him? *He* did not care. He swung his big fist like a sledgehammer, and Dr Hyssop went sprawling backwards with a startled cry, and landed in the shallows of the river.

The Hunter snatched the spear from him. He planted one hoof on Dr Hyssop's chest and snatched the horn too. As he turned from the river, examining his prizes, Dr Hyssop went floundering on his bottom through the water, calling out, 'Master! You don't understand! I come to serve you! I am not like that other man you spoke with, that fool Inshaw. I am like you! I have waited so long to witness you in your glory . . .'

The Hunter was not listening. He was gazing up at the spearhead as it glowed like a flame in the light from the fire. And as he gazed, so he changed. His grey hair took on a darker hue; the lines of weariness on his strange face faded. He shook himself, and stood even straighter; even taller. He raised his head and let out a fierce, stag-like roar that echoed through the forest.

'I will return to the woods of men and make them wild again,' he said. His voice was loud and deep and he spoke each word with care, for his mouth was made for ripping flesh, not forming words. 'I will hunt down the thief who stole my strength and trapped me here. I will sound my horn, and rouse my dogs, and the world will know the terror of the hunt again. And you, little man, with your mumbling and squeaking, you shall know it before all the rest.'

'But I . . .' whimpered Dr Hyssop, pulling himself up soggily onto the far bank of the river. 'But you . . . You can't!'

The Hunter tossed his antlers and let out a shout of sheer dark joy. He raised the old carved horn that Mrs Raftery had found beneath her rose-bed, and set it to his lips. Its voice went echoing through the woods, a bellow like an outraged bull that shook the crags and rolled away between the trees and echoed back from distant wooded hillsides in time to meet a second blast, and then a third.

'Oh, what is this?' whispered Will, crouched behind Utterly in the entrance to the holt. 'Oh, what new devilry is this?'

Around the Hunter's hooves, a mist was rising. It crept up out of the cracks and hollows of the ground in prowling clots that slunk and curled about. The clots were dog-like in some way Utterly couldn't really explain, until suddenly she realized that they really *were* dogs, not mist at all. Big, smoke-coloured hounds, with blood red ears, and black eyes, and low growls rumbling behind fences

191

of sharp white teeth. They swung their thick tails to and fro, and looked up longingly at the Hunter, awaiting his command.

Across the river, Dr Hyssop tremblingly raised his hands. His white face was whiter than ever, which made his red hair look redder still. He started to stammer out some plea for mercy, but the Hunter roared, 'Run, little fox.'

The vicar turned with a shrill scream and went scrabbling up the steep bank on all fours. He vanished into the shadows beneath the trees, and the Hunter stood laughing for a moment. Then he raised the horn again and blew one, thunderous, blast. His hounds put up their heads and howled, and as the echoes faded, they went streaming like grey smoke across the water, following the hot, fresh stink of Dr Hyssop's fear as if it were a red thread leading into the trees.

The Hunter slung the horn over his shoulder, gripped his great spear, and sprang after them.

Utterly and Uncle Will stayed in the shadows for a time, while the belling of the hounds and the crashing and rustling of the Hunter's progress through the trees slowly faded, until only the sounds of the river remained. Then Utterly took hold of Uncle Will's hand again, and they ran quickly to the fallen tree where Figgy Dan and Miss Inshaw were waiting to welcome them.

'Mr Dark,' said Miss Inshaw, recalling her manners

and making a ragged curtsey. 'This is Figgy Dan, and I am Elizabeth Inshaw.'

'Miss Inshaw,' said Will, bowing. 'I was told you had been struck by lightning.'

'Then you were misinformed, sir,' said Miss Inshaw, 'for I am sure I should have remembered such a thing.'

'Lord save us, Miss Utterly,' said Figgy Dan, 'I thought you were both dead 'uns when *he* came home. It was a stroke of luck, that clerical gent showing up when he did. But what did he want to go and give him back his spear and trumpet for? Why did he do such a thing? Weren't *he* fearful enough already, without giving him a spear to spike us on and a bloomin' trumpet to summon up his hellhounds?'

22

THE WILD HUNT

Utterly, Will, Figgy Dan and Miss Inshaw scurried up the steep paths that led out of the cleave. Sometimes, as they went, they heard the hounds on the far side of the river, and once, the horn rang out again. They were glad it was Dr Hyssop being hunted and not them, but they all felt certain Dr Hyssop could not evade those dreadful hounds for long, and feared that once he had been torn apart the Hunter might come looking for fresh prey.

This, thought Utterly, was how the mice who lived at Sundown Watch must feel, when Tab the cat was prowling.

'Miss Utterly,' said Figgy Dan, as they came panting to the top of the cleave, 'Do you still believe you can find us a way out of these dismal thickets?'

Utterly took out her stone with the fossil fish. She cupped it in her hands and held it before her as if it were a compass. For a long and worrying moment it seemed to be only a stone after all. Then she sensed the faintest tug that told her where its other half lay, out in the daylight on Barrowchurch Knoll.

'It is that way,' she said.

Uncle Will picked her up and set her on his shoulders so they could move more quickly, and off they went, moving swiftly in single file along the narrow paths that threaded through the trees. The high clamouring voice of the hound-pack drew nearer and then moved away, but it never entirely faded.

'They are still pursuing the wretched Hyssop,' said Will.

'I am surprised he has lasted this long,' said Figgy Dan.

'It serves him right, the infamous villain,' said Miss Inshaw tartly. 'Did you not hear the way he offered to betray all of humanity?'

'I suppose the poor wretch thought the Hunter would reward with him power and glory,' said Will. 'Like when Napoleon made his own brother King of Spain.'

'Well it is most improper behaviour for a member of the clergy. If we are ever able to find our way out of here, I shall be writing to the bishop in the very strongest terms.'

'I think them hellhounds are going to punish Hyssop fiercer than any bishop could,' said Figgy Dan.

They hastened on, through that eternal twilight in which the vast trees reared up like shaggy black columns. It seemed to Utterly that they were drawing near to the stone door, although she could not have explained in words how she knew that. But just as she was allowing herself to feel a little hope, there was a disturbance in the bracken away to their left, as if some unseen creature were rushing through it towards them.

Miss Inshaw raised her wooden spear, and Figgy Dan sprang bravely between her and the danger, growling a fearsome growl. Will set Utterly down and shielded her with his body, for he felt ashamed that she had put herself in peril to rescue him, and he was determined to set things right by protecting her, as a guardian was supposed to.

The crashing grew louder. The bracken thrashed and flailed and disgorged something panting and wild-eyed that they would all have thought was some terror-struck wild animal if it had not worn the tattered remnants of a good black coat.

'Oh stop!' warned Will, as Miss Inshaw lunged forward with her spear. 'It is only Dr Hyssop! You do not want a punctured vicar on your conscience, Miss Inshaw. Even if he is a dastardly one.'

Dr Hyssop stared at him, then at the rest of them, apparently too winded to speak. He was in a dreadful state, his clothes torn, his face slashed by thorns and smeared with blood and sweat and soil. He leaned against a tree and took shuddering gulps of air until at last he was able to say, 'I waded across the river, and so threw the brutes off my scent.'

'They will find it again soon enough,' said Miss Inshaw. 'Away with you, sir, or you will bring them down on us, too!'

'No,' said Will. He held out his hand. 'You must come with us, Dr Hyssop. However shabbily you have behaved, we cannot leave you to face the Hunter alone. We shall take you with us to the stone door.'

'How chivalrous of you, Dark,' said Dr Hyssop, with a kind of twisted smile. 'How very Christian. You do know that sort of high-minded charity has no place in this world? Indeed, it will have no place in our own world either once the Hunter rules again. In his kingdom there is but one commandment: that the weak must perish, and the strong survive.'

'We are all weak, compared with *him*,' said Figgy Dan.

'Speak for yourself, vagabond. I am one of nature's predators too. I am astonished the Hunter did not realize that he and I are kindred spirits. I should have addressed him in Latin, or some still older tongue . . .' Dr Hyssop shook his head, as if to clear away the thoughts that had been tumbling and tangling there all through his dreadful flight from the hounds. 'You will never find the stone door anyway, you prize fools. There is no escape from this place.'

197

'But find it we shall, sir,' said Will. 'Utterly, whose talents I gather you have already used for your own ends, will find a way for us.'

Dr Hyssop seemed to have no retort to that. He stared thoughtfully at Utterly, as if recalling how easily she had led him to the Hunter's spear.

Utterly looked down at the stone in her hands, and felt the tug or whisper of it, urging her uphill to where its other half was waiting. 'It is not far now, sir,' she said.

Dr Hyssop laughed. He made an elegant bow and said, 'Then lead on, Miss Dark.'

But almost as he spoke, the cry of the hounds broke out again, very loudly and not far off. 'You have led them directly to us, you bad, bad man!' wailed Miss Inshaw.

Dr Hyssop caught Utterly by the wrist and twisted her hand backwards until her fingers lost their grip. He wrenched the stone out of her grasp, and ran away into the dark.

'Come back!' wailed Utterly. 'My stone! My fish!'

'You unspeakable coward, sir!' shouted Will.

'You are a discredit to the cloth!' fluttered Miss Inshaw. 'I shall see you defrocked for this, sir!'

They ran after him, but the path rose in a series of steep zig-zags, and roots and brambles stretched across it as if they had grown there with the express purpose of tripping people. Miss Inshaw fell with a cry, and while

Will and Figgy helped her up, Utterly looked back and saw the hounds flowing like a mist through the trees on the slope below them.

'We cannot outrun them!' Miss Inshaw sobbed.

'There!' shouted Figgy Dan, pointing to an outcropping of rock that rose among the trees a little way off. 'We'll make our stand on higher ground.'

Will picked up Utterly again and ran after Miss Inshaw and Figgy to the rocks. They scrambled up among them and turned at bay there, but they had only Miss Inshaw's spear to defend themselves with, and there were so, so many hounds; a shocking number. They surrounded the rock till it was just an island in a heaving sea of hot bodies and bared fangs. Their long tails swayed, their breath smouldered, and they shouted and clamoured that they had their quarry cornered. From far off – but not nearly far off enough for Utterly's liking – they were answered by a single blast of the Hunter's horn.

The sound struck despair into the hearts of the little group upon the rocks, but it made the hounds howl for joy. Their master had heard them, and he was coming to make the kill.

'Utterly,' said Uncle Will, placing his hand on Utterly's shoulder and leaning down to her so she could hear him over the baying of the pack, 'I shall help you up into that tree there, and we must hope that when the Hunter comes he will be content with the rest of us, and leave you be.'

'But even if he does,' said Utterly, through tears, 'I do not want to be left alone! And besides, how will I ever find my way out, now that wicked old Hyssop has stolen my stone fish?'

Uncle Will had no reply to that. While he tried to think of one, the baying of the hounds grew even louder, as if some new frenzy had gripped them.

A figure burst from the trees, big and wild, wading through the pack, which parted like the Red Sea to let the newcomer approach the rock. Any that did not get out of the way swiftly enough received a fierce swipe with a hazel switch, which sent them yelping away with their tails between their legs.

'That is not the Hunter!' said Utterly.

'It is a monstrous woman!' said Miss Inshaw fearfully. 'The Hunter's mate perhaps, some dreadful ogress . . .'

'It is my wife!' cried Will. 'But how . . . ? Aish! I say! Aish!'

Aish gave a merry laugh, and vaulted up onto the rocks. One of the hounds sprang after her, baring his white teeth to tear out her throat, but Aish threw down her hazel switch, snatched Miss Inshaw's spear and, turning with it, let the hound's own weight drive it deep into his chest. She swung the brute above her head and dumped him down in ruin on his friends, who scattered backwards until they were just moon-bright eyes watching in silent fear from the dark between the trees.

Aish pulled Will into her powerful hug. Behind her, a smaller, nimbler figure came springing up between the rocks. 'Egg!' shouted Utterly. 'What are *you* doing here?'

'Rescuing you, of course,' said Egg. 'What do you think?'

'But however did you come into the Underwoods?'

'There is no time to explain all that,' said Aish. 'The Hunter is near. His dogs fear me, but he does not, and I do not wish to meet him if I can help it. Let us leave quickly by your stone door.'

'We cannot reach it,' said Utterly. 'Because that Dr Hyssop has stole my fish . . .'

'Fish?' asked Aish. 'Why, Utterly Dark, you have no need of fish. You have found the door already. Look, there it is, just yonder.'

She pointed uphill, and sure enough, there it was, although Utterly was certain there had been nothing but trees an instant earlier. Now three stones stood there, two upright and a third resting across their tops to make a lintel. In the space they framed, Utterly could see the pale grey light of day.

'Go quickly now,' said Aish. 'Yes, even you, Will Dark, you cannot help by lingering, though it is very brave of you.'

They did as she commanded, hurrying between the trees towards the light, while Aish remained upon the rocks to make sure the hounds remembered their manners. The blood of the one she had killed speckled her face and arms. She rubbed at a splash that had fallen on her sleeve, hoping her dress would not be spoiled.

When she looked up, the Hunter was watching her. He stood among his hounds with his spear in one hand and his horn in the other. Steam rose from him, and his eyes shone. So did the blade of his spear. Aish felt glad Will and Egg and Utterly were not there to see how scared of him she was, or how small and weak even she looked next to the strength and beauty of the Hunter.

He came slowly towards her, his hounds swirling round his legs like smoke. The one Aish had slain became a curl of grey vapour, and then a living hound again.

'Aish,' the Hunter growled.

Aish sprang down from the rocks and ran as fast as she could, uphill to where the others were squeezing themselves between the stones and out into the grey daylight on Barrowchurch Knoll.

23

THE WAY THROUGH
THE WOODS

Ted Beard's yawl had run all night under full sail with a sweet east wind behind her, and come in sight of Wildsea in the hour after sunrise. Captain Varley took her in to the old tin miners' quay at Stannary, and from there Egg went hurrying over the hills to Sundown Watch. He was knocking on the door before the Skraevelings and the Dearloves had finished breakfast.

'Why, Egg!' they said, as he burst in. 'What's this? What's wrong? Where's Will? Where's Utterly?'

'If you'll all stop asking silly questions, I might be able to answer some of 'em,' said Egg. 'But first I must talk to Aish. Is she at the Dizzard still? If I could borrow your horse, Reverend Dearlove, I could get there sooner.

There's shenanigans afoot on Summertide, and they're the sort of shenanigans only Aish knows how to sort out.'

'But Aish is not at the Dizzard!' cried Mrs Dearlove. 'She is here at Sundown Watch!'

And so she was. She was walking in the gardens, wearing the cashmere shawl that the Dearloves had given her for a wedding present, looking like a painting with her rusty hair tied back and the blue sea behind her. She had found to her surprise that she felt lonely in her house at Dizzard Tor, and lonelier still upon her lake isle, so she had come to Sundown Watch, where the bedclothes still held the faint scent of Will. ('Though I'm sure she is only imagining that, for they were laundered well enough.' said Mrs Skraeveling, who thought such Romantic notions reflected badly on her housekeeping.)

She was as astonished as everyone else when Egg appeared, and watched him with deepening concern while he said, 'Aish, you got to come with me. Will Dark's gone mucking about with some old magic out on Summertide and got himself lost inside a hill, and Dr Hyssop has made off with Utterly. Captain Varley brought me here in Ted Beard's yawl, and he's waiting in Stannary Bay to take us back.'

'Slow down,' Aish told him. 'Who is Ted Beard? Who

is Dr Hyssop? And what do you mean, my Will Dark is lost inside a hill?'

She got the story out of him in pieces, and slowly fitted them together until they made a sort of sense. 'I did not know,' she said. 'I have been such a goose. I felt it here on Wildsea, but I did not know the Hunter's power still lingered on the other isles. I did not know there were still any other entrances left to his wild forest . . .'

'Well there is,' said Egg, 'and Will Dark found one. But you can make things right, Aish,' he assured her, because he did not like seeing her look so worried, and hated hearing her call herself a goose. 'I had an idea, and Captain Varley reckons it's a good 'un. I know how you don't like leaving Wildsea . . .'

'It is not that I do not *like* leaving it,' Aish said. 'I cannot. I am of the land, not the sea.'

'Ah, but what if you was to take the land with you?' said Egg proudly. 'What if Mr Skraeveling digs up a load of turfs, and we spread them out like a lawn in the bottom of Ted Beard's yawl? Then you can go all the way to Summertide and never have to take your toes out of the good green grass of Wildsea till the minute you step ashore.'

Aish laughed. 'Oh, Egg, that is a most ingenious idea. I should love to travel like that, upon a floating garden! But how long would it take us to reach Summertide?'

'We could get the yawl grassed over by midday I reckon,' said Egg, who fancied himself something of an authority on nautical matters now. 'And with the wind in this quarter, going tack-on-tack, we should be at Summertide Town before midnight, and Barrowchurch this time tomorrow.'

'But all that time my poor Will Dark will be in danger. And who knows what will become of dear Utterly?' Aish shook her head. 'No, Egg. There is a quicker way, although it is more dangerous.'

Egg was annoyed that his clever plan had been dismissed. 'What will you do then? You mean to flap your wings and fly to Summertide, I suppose?'

'I shall walk,' said Aish.

'Across the sea?' Egg ran after her as she began striding back to the house. 'All right then. I'll walk with you. And don't tell me it's too dangerous,' he added, as Aish turned to tell him it was too dangerous. 'It would be more dangerous if you left me here, not knowing if Utterly was safe and not being able to lift a finger to help her, because if I was left here like that I would probably go mad with the worry of it, and starve to death or something.'

'Well, we could not have *that*,' said Aish, smiling at him. 'Very well, you shall come with me, and I shall be glad of you.' She stepped through the open French windows into the drawing room calling out, 'Mrs Skraeveling! There is a boy here in danger of starving, will you see if there is any breakfast left over for him? And perhaps someone would ride over to Stannary later and tell Captain Varley my compliments, but I shall not be needing him to carry me to Summertide . . .'

'Whatever is going on?' Mrs Skraeveling asked, coming out of the dining room with the others as Aish brushed past them and started up the stairs.

'Egg will explain while he eats,' said Aish, from the landing. 'I will be ready to set out just as soon as I have changed my clothes.'

She climbed on. The others turned to look at Egg.

'I will need a cake too, Mrs S,' he said. 'It ain't for me, honest. I promised one of your cakes to a sort of friend of mine.'

❖

The tide was out, baring the sand in Marazea Bay. Aish and Egg walked north along it as if it were a road. Aish had changed into her old russet dress and hung all her charms and talismans around her neck again. Egg carried a knapsack containing a fruit cake with almonds on the top. ('Which you're lucky it was in the larder,' Mrs Skraeveling had told him crossly, 'because t'ain't like I can just magic up cakes to order.') He still did not know where he was going, but he was content to follow Aish. He had been following Aish around for years, and she had never yet led him into any trouble she had not been able to get him out of.

As they walked, she made him tell her all he could remember about Barrowchurch. He told her every detail, from the strange objects in Dr Hyssop's cabinet of curiosities to the colour of the paint in the servant's quarters at the Grange. Even so, the walk proved longer than the story, and they went the last part in thoughtful silence until they had crossed the Trollbrook and were climbing up through the Dizzard woods.

Then Aish asked, 'Have you your pocket knife about you, Egg?'

'Course I have.'

'Then cut me a good, strong switch of hazel,' she said. 'From there at the cliff's edge where the trees are salted by the sea-mist and the spray.'

Egg did as she asked. She took the switch from him and swished it as they climbed on through the woods. They skirted Dizzard Tor and went down by steep secret paths until they came to a place Egg had never seen before, among the crags at the end of High Tarn.

It was not much of a place. Just tumbled rocks and a few struggling oak trees. A cleft opened in the base of the crag like a narrow door, with a lot of strings and trinkets strung across it. While Aish cleared the strings aside, Egg examined the carvings on the rock walls. Time had blurred them, but he could make out a pear-shaped woman with big bullfrog eyes, and a figure with antlers who held a spear in one hand and a curved horn in the other.

'That looks like the giant at Barrowchurch,' said Egg. 'Except for the horn and the spear and the hat-rack on his noggin.' He glanced at Aish. 'Ain't you wearing your antlers? You usually do, when there's magic stuff to be done.'

Aish shook her head. She had grown unusually serious. 'No antlers and no ram's horns today,' she said. 'Where we are going, it would be too easy to forget who I am, and come to think I really was a deer, or a sheep. That is why I am letting you come with me, Egg. To help me remember myself.'

Egg peered past her into the opening. It did not seem to go very far back into the rock. But then, as Aish removed the last of the string barriers and stepped in, it suddenly became a passage, stretching away into some immense, green distance. It had not opened in front of her; it was more as if it had always been a passage, and Egg had simply been looking at it wrong.

'Is this another door then? Like the one Will Dark went in at Barrowchurch?'

'It is different, but it leads to the same place.'

'What place is that?'

'A place that is the idea of a forest. It is very old, and very dangerous, and the Hunter who rules there is very powerful. He has been asleep, but I have felt him stirring these past months, and I think he is wide awake now.'

'You needn't be afeared of no old Hunter, Aish. I'll keep you safe. Just wait till I see him; I'll punch him on the nose.'

'Thank you, Egg. But you could not reach the Hunter's nose. He is exceeding tall.'

'Then I'll kick him in the whiff-whaffs,' said Egg, 'and punch his nose when he doubles over.'

Aish put her hand on Egg's small shoulder. 'Egg, if you see the Hunter, promise me you will run. Do not think you can fight him, because no mortal thing can stand against him. Do not think he will take pity on you because you are young and brave. The Hunter comes from a time before pity had been thought of.'

'I promise,' said Egg. Aish was so serious that for once he did not pretend to be disgusted when she stooped and kissed him on the forehead. He checked his knife was in his pocket, patted the cake in his knapsack, and went after her into the opening.

And at the end of the passage were woods deeper and darker than any woods Egg had ever imagined. There he and Aish wandered for hours, following scents the wind brought to her, and tracks she found in the soft places, until they heard three blasts of a horn come ringing through the trees. Aish nodded as if she had been expecting it. She began to stride towards the source of the sound so determinedly that Egg had to run to keep up, and it was not too long before they saw ahead of them an outcropping of rocks, and their friends surrounded there.

24

SWIM WITH ME

They scrambled out through the stone door and half ran, half tumbled down the steep side of the Knoll. Utterly and Egg, Miss Inshaw and Figgy Dan, Uncle Will, and then, after a long, breathless pause, Aish. While the others stood blinking in the daylight, startled to be safe, Aish began taking off the charms and pendants that she wore and stringing them between the roots of the oak so that they hung across the stone door. She whispered to herself as she worked, in words that none of the others could quite catch, and somehow, while they were distracted, the door vanished, and there were just roots where it had been, with a cat's cradle of knotted strings stretched across them, decked with holed stones, small skulls and curious little leather pouches.

'Will that seal the way?' asked Will. 'Is the Hunter locked inside?'

'I do not know,' said Aish. 'I should hope it, but he has grown strong, almost as strong as he used to be when . . .'

'When what?'

But Aish shook her head and looked away. She seemed shy of her husband. Perhaps she was just conscious of the hound's blood on her face and clothes, or felt naked without her necklaces and charms. But when Will reached out his hand to her she took it gladly, and kissed it, and said, 'I am so sorry I sent you to this place, Will Dark, and I am so very glad Egg came to fetch me before it was too late. How strange it feels to be on another island. Here are earth and trees and grass and stones and weather, just like Wildsea, yet it does not feel like Wildsea at all.'

'Egg fetched you?' said Will, and while Aish explained to him, Egg told the same story to Utterly.

Miss Inshaw and Figgy Dan, meanwhile, sat in silence, a little way apart. They had grown so used to one another's company in the Hunter's woods, but now that they were back in Barrowchurch, and Figgy Dan was no longer a dog, they were not quite sure how they should address one another. Figgy turned his head this way and that, and pricked up his ears, as if he had not quite shaken off doggishness yet. He was listening for his guns, which he had not heard since he stumbled through the door into the Underwoods. And, sure enough, there they were, booming and grumbling. But he thought they seemed quieter now, and compared with the terrors he had just escaped, they did not seem so very terrible after all; just someone moving the furniture about in distant rooms.

Over their sound, he caught another: a voice that called, 'Cousin Will? Miss Dark? Oh, Heaven be praised! Lizzie!'

It was Francis Inshaw, hurrying up the side of the Knoll with Mr Landover the butler and two of the male servants from the Grange. The servants carried stout sticks, and Mr Inshaw had a gun on his shoulder. He scrambled to where his sister stood, looked her up and down as if he could not quite believe that it was really her, and took off his coat so that she might wrap it around herself and hide her poor, torn clothes. 'Oh, Liz!' he said, with tears running down his face, 'I thought you was lost for ever! Hyssop said he would free you, but I fear I doubted him . . .'

'And you were right to, Francis!' said his sister. 'That mumping villain had no intention of freeing anyone, he was only interested in furthering his own beastly ends. Why, even when we tried to help him he stole Utterly's magical stone and . . .'

'Blast! Then I should have stopped him. I wish I had. He passed us a few minutes ago, running away from the Knoll with his clothes in disarray and a wild look in his eye. We tried to make him explain himself but he would only call us unpleasant names and cry, 'He is coming, he is coming!' He looked as though he had seen a ghost.' A nasty thought occurred to Mr Inshaw. '*Had* he seen a ghost, Lizzie?'

'Worse than a ghost, sir,' said Aish, coming down from the place where the door had been.

'Allow me to present my wife,' said Will.

'Why, 'pon my word! Mrs Dark! How came you here? And is that blood all over you! Dear lady, I trust you are not hurt?'

'Oh, it is not *my* blood,' said Aish reassuringly. 'We have been having adventures in the wild woods. But we have come safe out of them, thanks to Utterly and the Egg.'

'The Egg?' said Mr Inshaw, blinking at her.

'We think it's short for Egbert, sir,' said Utterly, and added, 'Ow!', for Egg did not like people knowing his real name, and had jabbed his elbow into her ribs in an effort to stop her saying it.

'Then I am indebted to you both,' said Mr Inshaw. 'But what am I thinking? We must get all of you back to the Grange. You all look quite done in. You will need warm baths, brandy, wholesome food. John,' he told one of the footmen, 'ride over to Swaylebury and ask Dr Collins to come. And Robert, tell Mrs Kakewich we shall need nourishing soup, and possets and the like.'

'We are not invalids, Francis!' said Miss Inshaw. 'Indeed, I have never been fitter. Figgy Dan and I have been living by our wits in a forest as wild as any in a fairy tale. We are not ill, but we are hungry. I for one could eat a horse.'

'An actual horse, miss?' asked Robert. It had been a strange day in Barrowchurch, and nothing would have surprised him.

John, Robert and Mr Landover hurried briskly away. The others started to make their way down the Knoll at a more leisurely pace, discussing menus and miraculous escapes.

Before she followed them, Utterly went to where the door had been and groped among the roots there for the other half of her stone. She found it easily enough, and ran her finger over the ridged impression of the fish. It was a beautiful impression, but it was not as beautiful as the fish itself had been. She wondered where that half had ended up – in thieving Dr Hyssop's pocket, probably, and halfway to Summertide Town or Wavering by now.

She stood up, pocketing the stone, and was about to run after the others when something else caught her attention.

'What is it?' asked Egg, who was waiting for her on the path, and had seen her stop and stare.

'Aish's charms,' said Utterly. 'Look! They are moving.'

'It is the wind.'

'What wind?'

Egg came to stand beside her, and together they watched the stones and other trinkets twirling on their strings. A hawk's skull ticked to and fro like a pendulum. A leather pouch dropped off its string and burst, spilling old teeth and tiny bones. Some of the knots were starting to come undone, slowly and hesitantly, as if clumsy invisible fingers were untying them.

'Well that ain't right,' said Egg.

'Aish!' they both hollered, hurtling down the side of the Knoll.

Aish, Will and the Inshaws had just reached the bottom and were walking out onto the common. Figgy Dan trailed a little way behind, as if he had suddenly remembered that in this world he was only a tinker, and not fit company for gentlefolk.

'I am starting to think I would have been better off staying a dog,' he said ruefully, looking round as Utterly and Egg ran up. 'I have got used to Miss Liz's company, and she to mine, but that can't be no more in this world, can it? I shall miss my time in those old woods, though I am glad we shall not have to fear the Hunter any more.'

'I think we shall,' said Utterly. 'I believe he is hunting us still. Aish!'

Aish stopped on the path ahead and turned. When Utterly caught up with her and explained what she had seen, her face grew very grave. 'Then my little wards cannot bind him any longer. If he can pass the stone door, he can come and go between this world and his wood just as he pleases. Now nowhere will be safe, not Summertide, nor Wildsea, nor even England . . .'

'It is all my fault,' said Utterly. 'It is because I found his spear. His power is greater now.'

'Hyssop would have found that old spear sooner or later,' said Aish, tousling her hair. 'And the Hunter would have broken free somehow. He has been a-worrying and a-poking his thoughts up into our world these many months. The storm gave him strength, so all this is the Gorm's fault in a way. Hyssop sensed his coming, and prepared a way for him, so it is definitely Hyssop's fault. And even my own happiness since I met my Will Dark, you may be sure the Hunter sensed that, and you may be sure he did not like it one bit'

'I think I felt him!' Utterly said. 'At the wedding – I did not know what it was . . . But Aish, why should your being happy make the Hunter angry?'

Aish glanced away. 'Why, I suppose it is because we are creatures of the same kind, he and I. It must vex him that I am happy and beloved, while he is prisoned in his nasty wood.'

'There is a sort of tightness in the air,' observed Miss Inshaw. 'As if another storm were approaching . . .'

'We should get under cover,' said Will. 'The Hunter's

hounds cannot come at us if we are within-doors.' He looked towards the Grange, a mile off on the far side of the river. Much closer, on the near bank, the chimneys of Nutcombe Lodge poked from its ring of trees. 'We should ask Mrs Raftery to shelter us.'

'We must not drag poor Jane and her mother into this business,' said Mr Inshaw.

'They are in it already, whether dragged or not,' said Aish. 'We must warn them of what is coming.'

❖

Dr Hyssop kept running until he reached the river. There he stopped, his terror fading a little. He glanced down at the stone he still clutched; the fossil fish, which had been his compass and shown him the way out of the Underwoods. For a moment he felt ashamed that he had snatched it from Utterly. Wanting to be rid of it, he walked down to the river bank and raised his hand as if to cast the stone out into mid-stream.

Then he changed his mind. It was clear the stone was some sort of powerful magical object, and clear too that he had much better claim to it than a mere child. He could feel the trees trembling at some force that was not the wind. He looked behind him, and saw the trees on the Knoll stirring too. 'The Hunter is coming,' he whispered. Thanks to him the Hunter had the power to leave the Underwoods again and pursue his quarry here, in the real world. So why had he not been rewarded?

'I showed too much politeness,' declared Dr Hyssop. He stood on the river bank with his body aching from his flight through the woods and his spirit smarting from the shame of his failure. His boot-heels sank into the soft earth at the water's edge, and he cursed himself for a fool. 'I should not have knelt before him. The old powers respect strength, not weakness. I should have told him, "Look here, my antlered friend, I'll give you your precious spear back, but these are my conditions . . ." Next time, I shan't run from him. I'll hold my ground, and offer him my terms . . .'

The trees went still, as if they had sensed some dreadful new development.

'The Hunter could not understand the things I told him of,' said Dr Hyssop, nodding his head firmly to help himself believe it. 'What can he know of roads and mills and cities, who has been trapped in that forest since the world was young? But when he gets out and sees them for himself, then he will come to realize that he needs Dr Hyssop at his side. All I shall ask in return is the chance to rule some small part of the world once he has reclaimed it for his own. Just England, perhaps. No – why be meek? Strength is what the Hunter respects. I shall demand all of Europe. He will need someone to take charge of the place while he goes hunting over the rest of the globe.'

Dr Hyssop slipped one hand inside his torn waistcoat, imagining himself a new Napoleon. The air was very still. Behind him in the river something made the faintest splash. Long green fingers snaked around Dr Hyssop's ankles, and a watery little voice said, 'Swim with me . . .'

25

GONE TO GROUND

Mrs Raftery was in her garden at Nutcombe Lodge, ruefully inspecting the damage done by that sudden flood the night before. Her rosy face grew redder still when she saw Francis Inshaw push the gate open. 'Mr Inshaw!' she cried, brandishing a broken fruit cane. 'I am surprised, sir, that you have the impertinence to show your face here! First you disappoint poor Jane, and then you let your blasted lake empty and wash out all me rose bushes! And what is this raggle-taggle band of vagabonds you are lettin' onto me property?' She stared at Utterly and Egg, Will and Aish, Miss Inshaw and Figgy Dan, who had all followed Mr Inshaw into the garden. 'They look as though they've bin dragged through a hedge backwards! I've a good mind to – oh, Good Heavens! What on earth is that?'

A thunderous roar came echoing across the garden, and the ground trembled. The trees on the Knoll all thrashed their heads in unison, and leaves whirled from them like a flock of birds rising, black against the grey belly of the sky. A wind took the leaves and swirled them towards the river, and as it struck the younger trees behind Nutcombe Lodge they gave up their leaves too, and the air was suddenly full of torn leaves and twigs and a wild howling that sounded almost like the baying of hounds.

'Is it an earthquake?' cried Mrs Raftery. 'Is it a whirlwind?'

'It is the Hunt,' said Aish.

'The Swaylebury hunt? But it ain't cubbin' season yet . . .'

'The Wild Hunt,' said Aish, towering over her. 'The Huntsman himself is coming, and terror runs ahead of him, and the wildness of the first woods comes behind.'

'Good Heavens!' said Mrs Raftery. 'Good Heavens above! Well, in that case, I suppose you had all better come indoors . . .'

They crowded behind her into the house, into the pleasant drawing room, where Jane Raftery set down her embroidery and blushed and tried not to look at Mr Inshaw while Mr Inshaw blushed and tried not to look at Jane.

'We must barricade the doors,' said Will, 'and shutter the downstairs windows. Aish, will guns work against the Hunter?'

'They will not, my love. But they might hold off his hounds a while, for they are mortal while they are in our world.'

'Jane, shutter the windows while I run to the gun-room,' ordered Mrs Raftery.

The house darkened as shutters were slammed one by one. It made everyone feel a little safer, but robbed them of any chance to see what was happening outside. They all hurried upstairs, trampling mud into Mrs Raftery's stair-carpet, and gathered at a landing window that looked out towards the Knoll.

'By Heaven!' gasped Mr Inshaw. 'It *is* an earthquake!'

Utterly pushed herself between Uncle Will and Aish and stood on tiptoe to peek over the high windowsill. The Knoll seemed to be collapsing in upon itself. Then it seemed to be exploding outwards – there was so much dust in the air above it, and the bare trees upon its sides heaved about so, and fell this way and that, that it was hard to tell what was happening. The church sank down into the roiling earth like a ship foundering in stormy seas. Then, for a moment, all was still.

Onto the Knoll's bare summit, where the church had stood so many years, there stepped an antlered figure.

'It is a black stag!' squeaked Jane Raftery. 'No – I am mistook – it is a man . . . a quite enormous man!'

The Hunter looked down across the waste of torn earth and tilted trees. He held his spear in one hand, his

223

horn in the other. The people who had carved his portrait in the chalk all those long centuries before would have known him instantly. He lifted the horn to his mouth and blew three blasts, and the notes went booming out across the Vale of Barrowchurch, and their echoes rang from the hollows of the downs.

Then, like grey smoke fuming from the vents of a fiery mountain, the Hunter's pack came pouring up out of the Knoll, solidifying into hound-shape as they rushed down through the shattered trees and out onto the common. The Hunter sprang down behind them.

'He is coming!' wailed Miss Inshaw.

'Terror runs ahead of him,' whispered Will, fighting the instincts that told him he should run and throw himself into the river rather than face the Hunter again.

Utterly tugged at Figgy Dan's sleeve. 'Mr Figgis – you were a soldier. What should we do?'

'Do?' Figgy Dan blinked down at her, as if to say, 'How should I know?' Then he drew himself smartly to attention and said, 'We must defend our position, miss.'

'How?' asked Aish. 'Command us, Mr Figgis – we are your army, though I fear we are but a poor one.'

'And I'm no general, ma'am, but I'll do my best. We shall need muskets in as many of the upstairs windows as we can manage, and the rest of us ready downstairs to fight off any dogs that make it through.'

'I have no muskets, sir,' said Mrs Raftery, panting up the stairs, 'but here is the old gun I use for shootin' vermin.'

Mr Inshaw threw the window up and leaned out with his own gun. The pack had reached the line of trees behind the house. Some of the hounds were casting to and fro for a way through the fence there, others just came straight over it and tore across the lawns towards the house. Mr Inshaw took aim at one, and fired. There was a spray of sparks, a startling quantity of smelly blue smoke, and a soft, damp-sounding bang. Mr Inshaw held the gun behind him, where Jane Raftery took it and set about reloading it with powder and shot that her mother had fetched from the gun room. Mr Inshaw produced a pistol from his pocket and took aim again. From a neighbouring room came the crack of Mrs Raftery's gun.

In the space between the gunshots another sound came drifting up the stairs: heavy bodies were throwing themselves against the shuttered windows on the ground floor.

'Downstairs!' yelled Figgy Dan. Will, Aish, Egg and Utterly raced after him. The shutters in the rooms at the back of the house were rattling under the impacts of the hounds, but none had got inside yet. Figgy Dan led the defenders to the kitchen, where a terrified cook and scullery maid were cowering. They ransacked drawers and cupboards, arming themselves with knives, broom-handles, anything that looked as if it might serve as a weapon. Utterly found herself a toasting fork. Egg equipped himself with a skillet he could hardly lift. Aish seized a cleaver and went running through into the drawing room, where the hounds seemed to be concentrating their attack on the French windows.

Will was about to her follow her when the cook, who seemed a highly strung sort of person, declared that *she* was not putting up with hellhounds, and that she was giving in her notice this instant and going back to her sister's place in Wavering. She had the back door unbarred before anyone understood what she was doing, and opened it before they could stop her. The hound which had been crouching on the doorstep knocked her sprawling and leaped over her into the kitchen.

The quick-thinking scullery maid slammed the door before any more could get inside. Figgy Dan, recollecting the smoky battlefields of his youth, ordered everyone to fix bayonets and form a square. He said it in such a commanding, sergeant-majorish sort of voice that they obeyed him without question and clumped themselves together in the middle of the kitchen, back-to-back. Utterly was afraid they had not so much formed a square as a sort of wobbly oval, but it was a wobbly oval that bristled with weapons, and that was the main thing. The hound prowled round it at a respectful distance, growling low and baring its yellow teeth, looking for a weak point to attack.

'Hold steady!' Figgy urged.

''Tis dripping its nasty old slobber all over my nice clean floor what I just mopped,' complained the scullery maid.

'I have seen smaller ponies,' said Will.

'I have seen gentler-looking tigers,' muttered Egg.

Utterly was about to point out that Egg had never seen any tigers at all, but just then the hound sprang at him. Perhaps it chose Egg because he was one of the smallest, and it thought his head would fit as neat as a walnut into the nutcracker of its jaws. But before it could seize him, Will jabbed it with his bread knife, Utterly poked it with her toasting fork, the scullery maid kicked it, and even the cook recovered herself enough to scramble up off the doormat and smack it smartly across the hind-quarters with a rolling pin. The hound forgot Egg and swung its head to and fro, turning to meet each new attack, until Figgy jammed his broom-handle halfway down its throat, and it gave up and fled whimpering into a far corner of the kitchen.

'He is not so brave now he ain't got all his friends with him,' said Egg, in a slightly shaky voice. 'I could see right down his gullet when he jumped at me,' he told Utterly. 'Like looking down a pink well, it was. I thought it was the last sight I'd ever see . . .'

Will and Figgy Dan herded the hound into the pantry, and had just shut the door on it when a crash and a cry from the other end of the house set everyone running to the living room. A hound had burst in through the window there, but Aish caught it as it scrambled in and lopped its head off with two blows of her cleaver: she was just dropping the body on the carpet when Utterly and the others came running to rescue her. Will dashed to the window to close the shutters again, with Figgy at his side in case more hounds came in. But the stretch of lawn outside the windows was empty, except for the bodies of a dozen hounds that had been shot by Mrs Raftery and Mr Inshaw from the upper floor.

'They've run away!' said Egg. 'We beat 'em!'

'It was a famous victory,' said Utterly, turning to beam at Figgy Dan.

'They have not gone far,' warned Aish.

They peered out through cracks in the shutters. The hounds had drawn back to the edges of the garden. They roved to and fro along the hedge line. Beyond it, their master moved between the trees, now as a man and now as a great black stag.

'If he thinks we are too tough a nut to crack, he may turn his attentions upon the Grange, or the houses in the village,' said Uncle Will. 'Oh, how I wish we had some way to warn them. They will not understand what they are facing, till the pack bursts in on them . . .'

'He will not trouble them,' said Aish.

'How do you know?'

'Because he knows that I am here.'

They all looked at her, wondering what she meant, but Aish seemed to have grown shy; she looked at the floor and told them nothing more.

Jane Raftery came trotting downstairs to say, 'Mr Inshaw's compliments, and there is something happening on the Knoll, which he thinks you should see, Mr Dark. Oh, lawks!' she added, as her eyes fell upon the hound Aish had killed, 'What a monster! And what quantities of blood it has spurted all over Mama's best Turkey rug!'

Will ran upstairs, and Utterly followed. Mr Inshaw was reloading his fowling piece beside the landing window. 'Look there, Will,' he said grimly. 'What was it your good lady wife said? 'The wildness of the first woods comes behind him . . .''

Will and Utterly went to the window. From this high vantage they could see the Hunter's pack surrounding the Lodge on all sides. Most of the dogs were sitting down, or lying in the long grass on the far side of the boundary, but all were alert, and it was clear that there was no escape through that ring of eyes and jaws. Beyond the hounds, their master strode to and fro, watching the Lodge with his cold, gold eyes. But those sights were not what had alarmed Mr Inshaw. He was pointing towards the Knoll.

A writhing darkness was gathering beneath the trees

there, and spilling out across the common, like lava pouring down the flanks of a volcano, except that this lava came in various shades of green. It was so strange to look upon that Utterly took a moment or two to understand what she was seeing. All around the Knoll, and spreading outward from it across the common and the river-meadows, full-grown trees were shouldering their way up out of the grass, as if they had been sleeping all along just under the turf, and the coming of the Hunter had aroused them.

The wild was returning to the Vale of Barrowchurch. It rushed towards Nutcombe Lodge like a green tide rising.

26

THE REWILDING OF NUTCOMBE LODGE

'What do you think, Cousin Will?' asked Mr Inshaw. 'Hounds were one thing, but we cannot shoot at trees. That is, I suppose we *can*, but I doubt we shall hurt 'em much.'

'It is the Underwoods,' said Utterly. 'They are pouring out into our world.'

'It is just an illusion,' said Uncle Will, doing his best to sound reassuring. 'The Hunter has conjured up a semblance of trees, to scare us.'

'No, Will Dark. Utterly is right.'

Aish had come halfway up the stairs, and stood there looking up at them. 'I know this Hunter,' she said. 'He is very old. He hates this world that people have made for themselves, with its bare hillsides and neat fields and stony houses. He is turning things back to how they used to be. Soon all this land will be just one wild wood again. It will be beautiful and cruel and there will be no place in it for people, except as his prey.'

She leaned against the wall, defeated. Will went down the stairs to take her hand. He did not ask her anything, but waited for her to say more when she was ready. The grandfather clock down in the hallway ticked and tocked. From outside came the restless creak and rustle of the new trees.

Lowering her eyes, Aish spoke again.

'I had another husband before you, Will Dark. Long ago, it was, and we were not wed in church, for churches had not been thought of in those days. Indeed, not many things had. I lived alone in my woods on Wildsea, and as I wandered singing there the Hunter heard me and he came to me. Strong he was, and handsome in his way. He had power over fire and stone and the bright metal that lies hidden in stone. He had made a spear for himself and poured his magic into it so that when he wielded the spear he grew more powerful even than he had been without it. He had a great love for the fury and the fierceness in things. And I had a great love for him, or at least I told myself I did. For I had felt the old Gorm's eyes watching me from out at sea, and I thought this bold Hunter could protect me from her.

'So we went on together well enough for a time, the Hunter and I. He would come to me on Wildsea for a while, and when he wearied of the hunting there he would summon his hounds and stride back through an opening he knew into that wider, wilder wood of his. I never followed him there, because it was not Wildsea, and because I did not love the hunt as he did. And when the seas froze, and human beings came across the ice and made their homes on Wildsea, well, I did not want to hunt *them*. They were too funny, too strange, too clever, too foolish, too sweet. I wanted to be friends with them.

'But not the Hunter. He thought people the best prey of all. Their terror when he chased them through my woods was sweet music to him. They were but animals who had got above themselves, he said, and it was his business to remind them of their proper place in the world. And best of all, they feared him so much they came to worship him, and carved his image in wood and stone, and he grew more powerful and more terrible than ever.

'So I began to tire of the Hunter, and he of me, I reckon, and he came less and less to my Wildsea woods, and I did not mind, for I had new friends now. But some-times when the moon was full, he would come barging and blustering up out of his hidden forest, and chase down my human friends. I told him they were precious to me. I told him of their stories and their songs, how kind they could be, and how wise. But there was nothing

I could tell the Hunter that did not make them seem even better prey. He only laughed at me, and then went chasing a young wood-wife who was dear to me. Summer was her name, in the language people used back then, and her laughter was like the underneaths of the leaves showing silvery all together when the wind blows through them. But to the Hunter she was just a thing to be chased, and he chased her to the land's edge, and in her terror she jumped from the high cliffs and died on the rocks below.

'That night, I went after the Hunter. I followed his tracks through that other world as if he was the quarry for once, and I the hunter. Down they led me into the dark cleave where he makes his holt, and in its inmost chamber by the mirror pool I found him snoring. He was tired from the chase, and sleeping deep. Quiet as a shrew, I crept to where he lay, and while he snored I took his spear. I took the horn he used to call his hounds. And I scurried back to my own Wildsea woods before he woke.

'But what was I to do with the spear and the horn? They were too powerful to be broken, and too dangerous to keep by me. I thought hard, and then I went and found the young man who had been my poor Summer's lover. Lorn was his name. In his grief he said he could not live on Wildsea any more, for every tree and stone reminded him of what he'd lost. He said he would hurl himself off the cliff too, but I told him it would be better if he lived and helped me make sure the Hunter never came hunting on my isle again. I gave the spear and horn to him, and said, "These things cannot be destroyed by any means I know, but get you on a boat" – boats had just lately been invented – "and take them as far as ever you can from Wildsea, and throw them into the deepest portion of the sea. Let the old Gorm have them, and let her guard them in the deeps till all worlds end."

'Lorn promised he would do just as I said. And when he had sailed away, I did set locks and wards and charms upon the entrance to the Hunter's world, and hoped that with his power so diminished by my thefts, he would not be able to burst out and trouble mine again.

'And he did not, and I forgot him. More springs and autumns came to Wildsea than I can quite remember, and the old Gorm distracted me with her rampagings, and new people came, and one day I found a young man lying on the shore, and thought, I am ready at last to take a new husband, and he shall be a gentler one this time.

'I did not ever think about that other young man, the grief-struck one of all those years ago, who had taken the Hunter's spear and horn away for me and promised to drown them in the deeps. It did not occur to me that Lorn might not have done as I had asked him. But I don't think he cast those things into the sea at all. I think he brought them here to Summertide.'

'He did!' said Utterly. 'Oh, he did! I saw him in my dream!'

'There, then,' said Aish. 'I suppose he left his grief behind him when he sailed away from Wildsea, and by the time he landed on this isle he was ready to make his life anew. So he told a tale that he had slain the Hunter, and taken his spear and horn as trophies. I expect he only told it to impress people at first, but he impressed so many of them that they made him their king, and when he died they built the Knoll over him. Poor silly man! But perhaps he remembered his promise to me at the end, and felt sorry that he had not kept it. And he told his people to bury the Hunter's spear and horn, thinking no one would find them.'

'And for a long time, no one did,' said Will.

'Ah, but the Hunter was listening and sniffing, trapped in his woody world, and Lorn's antics had drawn his attention to this place. Weak as he was, he forced his will up through the chalk. As the slow centuries turned his power filled the barrow where poor Lorn lay buried until it became a thin place, through which those with certain talents, at certain times, might pass between the worlds. Not the Hunter though; he could not come out; not yet. He was nothing without his spear. But more years passed, slow as great trees growing, and his strength increased, until . . .'

'*These* great trees ain't growing very slowly,' said Egg,

who had got bored with the story and turned back to the window.

Nutcombe Lodge was ringed now by a dense and tangled wood. One of the oaks erupting through the lawn had stretched out its branches almost close enough to touch the window, plunging the landing into shadow. Utterly ran to stand beside Egg. Peering down, she thought she saw the Hunter go striding between the trunks below.

'He is here!' she said.

'He has come for me,' said Aish.

'He still loves you?' said Will.

'Oh, the Hunter does not feel love. I tried to explain it to him once, and he did not understand one bit. He loves the strength in things, but he does not know love as you and I do, Will Dark. What he wants from me is his revenge. I stole from him, remember. I trapped him for all those long years. Now he wants to chase me down and stick me with his spear and keep my poor head as a trophy in his holt.'

'Why did you not tell us about him before?' asked Utterly.

Aish looked up at her, and gave a little sad laugh at her own silliness. 'Because I did not think of him. Because it was all so long ago. And because I did not want Will Dark to know how old I am.'

'I think I knew,' said Will. 'That is, I knew that you were someone . . . most uncommon.'

'You are not horrified then?'

'Only astonished,' said Will. 'And it is not the first time you have astonished me, and I doubt it shall be the last.'

'I fear it might,' said Aish. 'I had a feeling when I left my own Wildsea that I should not return, and now I am quite sure of it. For I cannot defeat the Hunter.'

A crack rang out, so loud and sharp that Utterly thought it was another gunshot. But Mr Inshaw and Mrs Raftery were the only ones with guns, and they were both stood on the landing behind her, listening to Aish and Will, and seemed as surprised by the noise as she.

'Mrs Raftery!' cried the scullery maid, from down below. 'Something untoward be happening to my parlour floor!'

Something untoward was happening to all the floors. The house filled with the creak and crunch of splintering boards as branches began pushing their way up out of the earth beneath. The flagstones in the hallway were shrugged aside by boisterous saplings that stretched and thickened into trunks and stabbed their heads up through the floors above. Cracks spread down the walls like ivy: ivy spread up the walls like cracks. Tough tendrils burrowed through plaster, dug into mortar, gripped stone and brick in woody fingers.

'Fall back! Everybody downstairs!' ordered Figgy Dan, and they scrambled to obey him, although the stairs themselves were heaving like a ship at sea as more greenery grew through them. Mrs Raftery shrieked, carried upward like a rider on a rearing horse by an oak that had sprouted from the very spot where she was standing. The trees forced their heads up through the roof, and plaster, lath and slates came raining down.

It was like watching a thousand years in the life of a forest compressed into a few short seconds, thought Utterly. And she wondered if that was what magic was, or much of it; something to do with time; a hurrying-up or slowing-down of nature, or a skipping back and forth to see what would be, or what had been long ago . . .

'Utterly, don't stand daydreaming there!' said Uncle Will, and dragged her with him into the dubious shelter of a door-frame just as a hundredweight of roof-slates smashed down upon the place where she had been.

'We must fetch Mrs Raftery down!' shouted Mr Inshaw, running to the foot of that lady's tree and wondering if he remembered how to climb trees – he had not done so since he was a lad.

'No, no, sir!' called Figgy Dan, above the grumble of shifting brickwork. 'The lady has the right idea! The enemy has breached our outworks, and his infantry will be upon us soon. Everyone climb, climb as high as ever you can!'

They began scrambling up into the newborn trees. Miss Inshaw hoisted herself into the branches with surprising nimbleness, having had plenty of practice during her stay in the Underwoods. Egg scampered like a monkey up the trunk of an ash. Figgy Dan hurried to the kitchen to help the cook and scullery maid up. Mr Inshaw found an oak so gnarled and lumpish that he could climb it like a ladder, then noticed Jane Raftery still wringing her hands in the hallway, and climbed gallantly back down to help her up it too. Uncle Will lifted Utterly onto a branch and told her to climb higher, then turned back to offer a helping hand to Aish.

But Aish shook her head. 'It is me he wants, Will Dark,' she said. 'He may forget about the rest of you, providing you stay quiet while I lead him away. And perhaps something may occur to stop him, though I cannot think what. I doubt there are many to match him for power or rage in this world of nowadays.'

'Aish, no!' said Will. 'I will not allow it!'

But Aish just smiled, and kissed him, and said, 'You are the best thing the sea ever washed up, Will Dark.' Then, before he could resist, she lifted him bodily up and hung him over the same bough Utterly was sitting on. 'Look after him, Utterly Dark,' she said. 'I am going to lead the Hunter the hardest chase he has ever known.'

27

BREAKING COVER

A few surviving windows burst with quick, startling sounds like icy sneezes – *tish, tish, tish*. Then, with a slithering groan, the whole rear wall collapsed. It was like being in a doll's house when someone opens it up to look inside, thought Utterly, as the leafy green daylight came dazzling in. And before the rubble had even settled, Aish sprang up onto the ruins of the wall and leaped down into the dark wood that had come crowding in where Mrs Raftery's gardens had been.

'Aish!' Utterly called after her, longing to do something, anything to help. Suddenly she remembered the half-stone in the pocket of her dress. As her hand closed upon it she felt again that great dark wave of understanding roll towards her, just as it had in the Underwoods, never quite breaking, but rippling with uneasy memories. The Gorm had far more power than any Hunter. Surely the Hunter would not dare touch anyone who carried a thing the Gorm had made?

Utterly had not climbed higher when Uncle Will told her to, so the bough she sat upon was still only around six feet above the floor. She slid off it, dangled, and let herself drop. Will called out after her in alarm, but she said, 'It is all right, Uncle Will. I am going to give Aish my stone, it will protect her!'

It had seemed like a rather brilliant plan when she was sitting upon the bough. Here at ground level, she began to see its flaws. She started to move back towards the tree, but a hound came running at her and she squealed and leaped aside. 'Utterly!' Uncle Will was shouting, from up in the branches. The hound heard him and threw itself against the trunk of the tree. Uncle Will snatched back the hand had been reaching down to Utterly just in time, and the mantrap jaws slammed shut on empty air.

But other hounds were all around, streaming through the green shadows into the ruins of Nutcombe Lodge. Since going back was quite impossible, Utterly went on, scampering over roots and ruins, praying the pack would be too busy baying at her friends to trouble her, praying that her friends were far enough up their various trees that the hounds could not drag them down.

'Here I am, Hunter!' Aish's voice called, from somewhere in the new woods. 'Come catch me if you can!'

Utterly climbed over the rubble of the fallen wall, and there ahead of her was Aish.

'Utterly! How came you here? Did you fall down from your tree, poor thing?'

'I came to help you, Aish,' said Utterly.

The horn sounded among the trees nearby, a single high, clear note. The hounds' rough music changed. The Hunter was calling them off, and setting them on new prey.

Aish hitched up her skirts and tied them round her waist, baring her strong legs so she might run faster. She scooped Utterly up and fled, with Utterly draped over her shoulder like a sack.

'What were you thinking of, Utterly Dark?' she panted as she went. 'Did you think perhaps the poor Hunter would not be fast enough to catch me, so it would be fairer if I had your weight to slow me down?'

'I – thought – I – could – help . . .' said Utterly, upside down, her face bumping against Aish's broad back with every word. She twisted herself around so she could speak more clearly. 'I brought my stone. Dr Hyssop took the half with the fish in, but I have the other, and it bears a perfect impression of the fish, so the Hunter will know it came from the Gorm, long ago. I thought he would be afraid of it, and let you be.'

Aish laughed merrily, and put her head down to race through the whippy lower branches of a stand of birch. 'Utterly Dark, the Hunter is not likely to be scared of a stone. We are miles and miles and miles from the sea. Your old Gorm has no power here. He will only laugh at you, and then he'll kill us both.'

Behind them, deafeningly loud, the Hunter's horn rang out.

'There,' said Aish. 'He is telling his doggies to leave our friends alone and find my scent. Or maybe' – she hurdled a fallen branch – 'maybe he has already found my scent for himself, and he is calling the pack to follow. I reckon' – she ducked under a low bough – 'he does not really need hounds at all. He just likes their nasty fierceness and the din they make.'

'Then I have made an awful mistake,' said Utterly. 'I meant to help, but I am just an encumbrance to you. You should put me down . . .'

'You are a sweet encumbrance,' said Aish. 'And no heavier than a couple of feathers.'

Light broke around them as Aish outran the trees and burst into fields where none had sprouted yet. A path wound uphill through ripening wheat, speckled with the crumpled silky scarlet heads of poppies. There was a wooden fence, which Aish vaulted with ease. 'I'll set you down when I can run no more,' she said, landing in long grass on the other side. 'Then I shall turn and face the

Hunter. He will want to make the most of his revenge, I expect, and that will buy you time to get away.'

They were on the grass of the open downs now. A hare went loping out of Aish's path. Utterly could not believe there would ever be a time when Aish could run no more. How could the Hunter or even his hounds keep up? But when she looked back she saw him stride from the wood's edge and start after Aish up the hill. His pack raced ahead of him. Behind him the ground rippled, and divots of earth filled the air, and the crowns of great trees came crackling up through wheat and grass. The wildwood spread behind him like a green cloak.

And now Utterly could feel Aish flagging. The ground was rising steeply and it was impossible to turn aside and seek a lower way without being cut off by the hounds. They were close now, and the voice of the Hunter was loud and laughing.

'Aish!'

Still Aish kept running, up, up, up the steep scarp slope, but so slow now that even Utterly could have overtaken her. Sweat soaked her dress and her breath came in shuddering gasps, and Utterly felt so, so sorry for slowing her.

And then suddenly the hounds were all around them. Aish stumbled. A hound caught her skirt in its jaws and Utterly heard the fabric rip. Another seized Aish by the leg. She cried out and went down on her knees and tried to rise and yet another hound slammed into her and knocked her sprawling. Utterly tumbled off her shoulder and rolled through grass and onto bare chalk with the stink and clamour of the hounds all around her.

The Hunter's horn rang out again, calling them to heel, quieting them. A wind whispered the grass-heads. Aish's breath came wracking out in sobs. Utterly got up on her hands and knees. She saw that she was back in the outline of the old chalk giant, on the curved white path that was his left shoulder. There was the hole that Dr Hyssop and Mr Inshaw had dug, only a few yards away.

And here was the Hunter, striding towards her up the slope of the hill with his spear in his hand. He had polished it since she saw him last, and its leaf-shaped blade shimmered with a beetly iridescence. Behind him, the Vale of Barrowchurch had become a forest, steaming with its own newness. The ruins of the mound and the ruins of Nutcombe Lodge were islands in a sea of trees.

'I command you by the power of the Gorm,' said Utterly, remembering the actual sea. She wished her voice did not sound quite so tiny, or so terrified. She groped for her stone and held it up in one small, shaking hand so the Hunter could see the imprint of the long-dead fish. 'This land was all sea once, Mr Hunter,' she said. 'The Gorm reigned here, and the land remembers her still. So kindly go back to your own woods, and leave us be.'

The Hunter made a grumbling sound of unease deep in his throat. He had run in the first woods when the world was young, but even those woods had an end, where the wild surf beat against the shore and the drift-logs were tossed about like twigs. From beyond that edge, far out in the deeps, the Hunter had felt the Gorm's gaze on him, and feared her. It startled him to hear her name from this frail-seeming human child, and to scent once more her deep sea magic. He was not afraid of Utterly, but he was at least unsure of her.

While he hesitated, Aish rose painfully to her feet and stood swaying. Her face shone with sweat and strands of her hair were stuck to it. Blood was twining down her leg from the gashes the hound's fangs had torn. It made a scarlet puddle on the chalk, with pale dust on its surface. 'I had hoped to lead you a longer chase,' she said. 'But Summertide is not my island, and my strength here is not nearly what it is in on Wildsea.' She smeared hair out of her eyes and nodded at Utterly. 'Leave this girl alone. The power of the sea is in her. You can feel it, can't you? She is the Gorm's favourite, and if you harm even one hair of her dear head you shall have the old Gorm herself to reckon with.'

The Hunter made his rumbling sound again. 'Enough talk. I came to hunt, not to talk.'

'He never was a one for conversation,' said Aish, winking at Utterly. 'That is one reason I like people better.'

'Run, Aish,' said the Hunter.

'I've run far enough.'

'Run, woman,' said the Hunter.

'Why? Is there no thrill to it if I just stand here?'

'Run,' said the Hunter, 'and I will not harm the child.'

Aish nodded, as if to seal a hard bargain. She glanced at Utterly again, and sort of smiled.

Then she turned and fled, with her hair flying out behind her. One limping stride she took; two; three – and the Hunter sprang after her, right over Utterly's head, with such speed that Utterly guessed he had been holding back before, running slowly to make the chase last longer. Now he was tired of it, and ready for the kill. He caught Aish by her flying hair and wrenched her off her feet. He slammed her down upon the ground so hard that Utterly felt it through the chalk.

'Aish!' she screamed, and flung her stone at the Hunter. 'Leave her! I command you! In the name of my mother!'

The stone had barely left her hand before she realized with a shock what she had said. She had not meant to. She had meant to say, 'in the name of the Gorm.' Why should it have come out as 'my mother'?

And then the wave that that had been building in her mind all through this long day broke over her. She remembered with a shocking clarity every detail of her visit to the Hidden Lands. She heard again the Gorm say, *I am your mother*. She remembered the log in which, with dreadful grammar, the Gorm had recorded how she came to have a human child, and swaddle her in a mermaid's purse, and leave her in Blanchmane's Cove for the Watcher on Wildsea to raise.

So that was what the White Queen had meant when she had recoiled from Utterly and called her 'Sea's Daughter' . . .

How could I have forgotten such a thing, Utterly wondered. But she had never really forgotten it. She had locked the memory of it in some basement part of her mind, deep beneath more ordinary memories. That was why she had kept talking to the sea at Sundown Watch, and why she had missed it so when she came to Barrowchurch. That was why she had felt that curious urge to swim away and find the Hidden Lands. She had known all along that the Gorm was her mother, but she had not been able to put it into words, or even think about it head-on. The knowledge of it had only returned to her when she stopped thinking at all, and let her anger and her fear take charge.

The stone hit the Hunter on his hairy back, and dropped into the grass. He did not even notice it. Aish was struggling to rise, but he pinned her to the earth and twisted her head back so her long brown throat was bared. He raised his spear. The blade gleamed, blood-hungry. The hounds howled. Aish was as still and staring as an animal that knows its death is near. The Hunter threw back his antlered head and bellowed his triumph at the sky.

And as Utterly stood watching, shocked and trembling, with her hands clenched into tight and useless little fists, a terrible rage swept over her. It was not even the Hunter she was angry at. He was quite a stupid character, and only doing the one thing he knew how. She felt more angry at herself for letting him do it, and at the Gorm, who had turned her back on Utterly. What was the point of being the sea's own daughter if the sea just sulked and let you be chased over hill and dale by mad stag-headed gods? Aish was a far better mother to her than the old Gorm had ever been, and now Aish was going to die, and Utterly was too small and scared to stop it.

'Mother!' she screamed, so loud it hurt her throat. 'Mother! Help me!'

And the Gorm heard her.

28

DEEP TIME

Those green hills had all been ocean once. In a way, they still were. Time meant very little to a being like the Gorm. Moments could last an age, while ages flickered by like moments. Yesterday, today, tomorrow: they were all one to the eternal Gorm. Utterly's cry of anguish echoed through the chalk to a time when the chalk was still a million, million animalcula swimming in a shallow tropical sea. It made their chalky shells ring like tiny white bells.

And the Gorm heard her.

Utterly felt the ground ripple beneath her. She looked down, and found she was seeing through the chalk again as if it were clear water. In its depths drifted a glittering dust of little creatures, riding the warm salt currents for a while before they died and sank.

And Utterly sank with them; down through the water, down through the ages, until she stood beneath a snowstorm of the falling creatures, upon a drift of their infinitesimal shells that was already miles deep.

The water was dim twilight at this depth, with restless sunbeams wavering in it. Through the twilight and the sunbeams, from some far distance, a speck of light appeared, and approached, and became a squid of immense size. It seemed made entirely of clear glass. Its heart and brain glowed like soft lamps deep in its transparency, while up and down its ten long arms little dancing firefly flakes of light went flickering, blue and pink.

Utterly curtseyed, as politely as she could. 'Good day, Mama,' she said.

'Utterly Dark,' replied the squid. It did not speak with its mouth, which was really more a sort of glass beak than a mouth, but just in Utterly's head, in a voice like the deep, rich note of an expensive violoncello. It rippled for a time as if it were trying to remember something. Then it folded in upon itself and shrank and became a woman in a white dress, whose long black hair trailed and swirled like inky tentacles upon the waters. It was the form the Gorm would wear millions of years hence, on the shores of an island that had not yet risen from the deep.

'I offered you so much, Utterly Dark,' the Gorm said, not troubling to move her blue lips. 'You are my own child, and I came to love you. But you spurned my love, and went back to the land.'

'I did not mean to be ungrateful,' said Utterly, looking down meekly at where the chalk-shells were piling up around her feet. 'I should have loved to stay in your Hidden Lands. In tore me in two to leave. But there are people on Wildsea that I love too. And now I need your help to keep them safe. It is the Hunter, he is going to kill Aish. And then he will hunt Egg and Uncle Will and all the others too, I expect.'

Behind the blizzard of shells the Gorm's eyes changed slowly, from one cold unkindly sea-shade to another. 'So the wood god is awake again?' she said.

'He has found a way out of his woods into the Vale of Barrowchurch, on the island of Summertide, in the year of our Lord eighteen hundred and—'

'Silence, child. These names mean nothing. Land is but a dream, that comes and goes like the foam upon a wave. Only the sea rolls on for ever.'

'Then why can't the sea help me?'

The Gorm considered. She looked up through aeons of time and fathoms of sea that would one day be stone, and saw Aish laid upon the surface, with the Hunter kneeling over her, and Aish's blood a red cloud spreading in the water.

'She is so little, that one. Her life is not much longer than a human life, and a human life is not much longer than the life of a bubble. She means nothing.'

'She means something to me,' said Utterly. 'And to Egg, too. And she means a great deal to poor Uncle Will.'

The Gorm's eyes kept up their restless cycle, grey to green, green to grey. She came closer to Utterly, looking down through the steady fall of shells. She touched Utterly's face with her cold hand. 'You must come to me,' she said. 'I can save her from the wood god. But in return for my help you must come to me, and dwell with me in the deeps, and walk with me among the Hidden Lands.'

It seemed such a little thing for Utterly to promise. The longing to see the Hidden Lands again had been in her anyway, ever since she'd left them. She would miss Sundown Watch, and Wildsea, and her friends, but what would become of Wildsea anyway if Aish were dead? What would become of Egg and Uncle Will?

'When spring comes again, I will go into the sea and find you,' she said.

'It is a promise then, and solemn?'

'Yes. It is a promise. But only if you save Aish from the Hunter.'

'What? You think I can't? A little buzzing god like that? He is nothing to me.' The Gorm brushed the hair back from Utterly's forehead, and looked gently at her for a moment. 'Until the spring then, Utterly Dark.'

A deep sea current flexed like a muscle. It lifted Utterly out of the knee-deep drift of shells and carried her up and up while the shells snowed down all round her. The pale upturned face of the Gorm faded against the pale plain below. Utterly rushed towards the shifting stained-glass surface of the sea, and burst up gasping through the back of a wave. Other waves heaved all around her, huge, slow and unbreaking, for she was in mid-ocean and there was nothing for them to break upon, just the endless swell lifting her up and down under a low grey sky.

Until slowly she began to see that the waves were not waves but hills, and their heaving motion was only a fading dream. The snow of shells had piled so deep that it had turned to chalk, and winds and weathers had smoothed and carved the chalk into downs, and grass had grown on them, and Utterly crouched upon the high slope of the hill above Barrowchurch, while the Hunter raised his spear over Aish.

But he did not strike. He looked up at the sky instead. There, white against the grey, gulls were wheeling, crying their long, sad cries. How had they come here, so suddenly, so far inland? There was a smell in the air that Utterly had almost forgotten. It was the salt smell of the sea.

The hounds whimpered. The Hunter forgot his prey and sprang up. He gripped his spear and turned this way and that. He sensed the approach of an enemy, but did not know from which way the attack would come.

Auk, auk, auk, screamed the gulls, blowing overhead on the salt wind. Utterly sensed a tremor deep in the chalk beneath her. The hounds sensed it too, and scattered, howling, tails between legs. The Hunter turned, and turned again, sniffing the sea air, scanning the horizons. He was feeling for the first time the fear his prey had known.

The land remembered it had once been water. Up through the turf behind the hunter burst a grey shape. Up through the turf in front of him burst another. They rose straight into the air, like two grey blades thrusting out of the earth. Shattered chalk tumbled from them like falling spray.

Utterly thought they were stones at first; two new standing stones sprouting here upon the down. They were grey enough for stones, and rough enough, and tall enough. But then they grew taller still, and she saw the roughness was just barnacles, and the grey beneath was skin. They were the jaws of a whale so big it could have eaten Jonah's whale for breakfast and still had room left for elevenses. Perhaps it had been a fossil like Utterly's lost fish, lurking in the hill all these centuries, waiting for its moment to rise and snatch the Hunter like a trout taking a fly.

The Hunter, trapped in the turbulence between its jaws, screamed out just once in rage and terror. Then the whale slammed its vast mouth shut on him, and white foam boiled out between its peg-like teeth. It was still rushing upward, driven by the energy that had carried it all the way to the surface out of some unimaginable abyss of time. It rose like a finned tower until its nose was up among the gulls, a hundred feet above the grass where Utterly cowered with Aish. Utterly saw its eye; a small eye for such a massive creature, and surprisingly low down on its flank. The eye burned grey, then green, then summer blue.

The whale toppled. A fan of spray burst up as it struck the surface. A massive fin carved downward through the turf. Waves heaved outward, lifting Utterly on their crests, pitching her into their troughs. She could not tell if it was earth or sea she rode on, but she struggled closer to Aish and they clung together and watched the grey curve of the whale's back arch out of the down. The flukes of its tail came up, flourished for a moment in the air, and then plunged through the grass, and were gone.

The spray that had been falling all around turned into powdered chalk, and blew away upon the breeze. The gulls went with it, calling, calling. Then all was quiet. The Hunter's hounds had vanished. A faint greyish haze of mist or smoke drifted over the grass where they had been, and quickly faded.

'The Gorm!' said Aish, in a disbelieving whisper. 'How did the old Gorm come here, so far from the sea?'

'This land was all sea once,' said Utterly.

'You called upon her, and she came . . .'

'She is my mother.'

'So you have remembered that! I wondered when you would.'

'Then you knew?'

'I guessed it.' Aish looked solemnly at her. 'Now, Utterly Dark, I hope you did not promise that old Gorm anything in return for helping me?'

'Nothing that I did not want to give,' said Utterly.

Which was true, she thought. Wasn't it? Because she had always known she would return one day to the deeps, and the Hidden Lands, and though her head had forgotten the Gorm was her mother, her heart had remembered it, just as the hills of Summertide remembered being sea.

And anyway, it was not as if she would be going yet; she was not going till spring came again, and that was ages away. So she had months and months and months to prepare herself . . .

The Hunter's horn and spear lay on the grass. The horn had split in two, and the spearhead had lost its beetlish sheen. Aish tore a length of fabric from her ruined dress and bound it tightly round her torn and bloody leg. She took the spear and leaned on it like a staff as she and Utterly went slowly together down the hill.

'Aish, is he dead, the Hunter? Can a thing like him die?'

'I am a thing like him, and I would be dead if you and your Gorm had not saved me. I expect that big old fish swam back with him to the time when all the world was water, where it can digest him at its leisure. So yes, he is dead all right, as dead as a doornail, and I for one do not feel too sorry.'

Utterly was not so sure. Not about not feeling sorry – she did not see how anyone could shed a tear for that black-hearted hooligan. But if the Hunter was dead in a whale's belly all those ages ago, how could he have menaced Utterly and her friends in the here and now?

But she was trying to make sense of it all, the way Uncle Will would, and if there was one thing she had learned from her adventures it was that magic did not make that sort of sense. Magic obeyed no rules, unless they were the rules of dreams, and dream-rules were not really rules at all.

For instance, she would have expected that vast new forest the Hunter had conjured to have faded away like his hounds, but it still filled the vale below her. And there, running out of the edge of the trees, was Uncle Will, and there was Egg behind him. And there was Mr Inshaw, and Miss Raftery, and Miss Inshaw and Figgy Dan, and Mrs Raftery, and her scullery maid, and even some of the servants from the Grange, all hurrying up the long slope of the down towards Utterly and Aish, and calling out their names.

29

NEW TIMBER

The new woods ended at the edge of the Swayle, so Barrowchurch Grange was much as it had ever been, although the view from its windows was strangely altered. Trees now covered the common entirely, all the way to the foot of the downs. The grey clouds that had hung over the valley for weeks were finally beginning to break up, and beams of sunshine found their way through to light up first this tree-top and then that, as if trying to draw attention to the prettiest ones.

The people who gathered on the terrace outside the drawing room that afternoon seemed strangely altered too, thought Utterly. She supposed anyone must be, who had brushed up against the old powers of the world. Mr Inshaw, despite his wild adventures, seemed happier and more at ease than she had ever seen him. While he had been sharing a tree with Jane Raftery he had taken the opportunity of explaining to her the reason he had broken off their friendship. She had understood, and forgiven him, and now they sat very happily together, holding hands.

Aish and Uncle Will were holding hands too, but they seemed less happy than before – the Hunter had hurt Aish's pride as well as her person, and as for Uncle Will, Utterly guessed it was one thing to tell people your wife is a goddess in human form, but rather another to find out for certain that she really *is*.

Utterly had only lately met Miss Inshaw, so she could not be sure she had been altered, but she seemed a far stronger and more sensible person than the lady who had written those whimsical diaries and gone out looking for Fairyland on the night of the great storm. And as for Figgy Dan, who sat nervously sipping tea out of the finest porcelain he had ever handled, Utterly could not imagine now how anyone had ever mistaken him for a dog.

And was Utterly changed? Well, she had found her way into the Underwoods and rescued Uncle Will, and called the Gorm out of time's deeps to save Aish, and those things made her feel almost frighteningly grown-up. And then there was the promise she had made . . .

'I reckon you and me are the only ones who have kept our heads through all these catastrophes, Utterly,' said

Egg, breaking in upon her thoughts. 'I don't rightly know what they'd have done without us.'

'It was very brave and clever of you, trusting the river girl and going all that way to fetch Aish,' said Utterly.

'Pffft,' said Egg modestly, but he knew she was right, and he helped himself to the last of the sponge fingers like a boy who had earned it.

'I do not know what shall become of us, I'm sure,' said Mrs Raftery, who seemed rather flustered and deflated by her adventures. 'Without a roof over our heads, and my garden all overgrown, and all our clothes and furniture spoiled, or stuck in the treetops, or scattered to the winds . . .'

'We shall rescue as much as we can tomorrow,' said Mr Inshaw. 'Then you and Jane must move here to the Grange. It is far too big a house for just me and Elizabeth. Jane and I shall marry, and you shall have the entire west wing for your own, till you find somewhere better. That is – unless Cousin Will is planning to stay long. *Are* you planning to stay long, Cousin Will?'

'Aish and I must go home to Wildsea as soon as she is recovered,' said Will.

'Which will be very soon,' said Aish. 'Your kindly Dr Collins said my leg was healing surprising quick. I think he was rather vexed. He had probably been looking forward to sawing it off.'

Miss Inshaw looked dismayed. 'I was hoping Mrs Dark

would stay a while, to preserve us from danger in case *he* returns, or *his* stone door should open again . . .'

'You do not need me,' said Aish. 'The Hunter is buried deep, and the door is shut. But it is true, your Knoll will always be one of the thin places, and someone should keep an eye on it. A caretaker as it were, to keep a look out for trouble, and stop learned gentlemen from poking their noses where they don't belong. I was thinking Figgy Dan might be the very person for that job.'

Figgy Dan tried to wag his tail, then remembered himself and nodded eagerly instead. 'Oh yes, ma'am. That would suit me about perfect, I reckon. For out here, despite all your kindnesses, I begin to hear my guns again, a-roaring and a-rumbling. But in the trees there are so many other sounds, so much creaking and stirring and rustling and *growing* going on, I cannot hear no guns at all. I reckon I could live peaceful in those woods. And when I am not engaged in a-watching for trouble, Mr Inshaw, I could maybe manage the wood for you – coppicing and such? For woods need care, and I know a bit about how to care for 'em, my old dad having been a woodsman himself.'

'Capital notion!' said Mr Inshaw.

'You shall be the Watcher on Summertide,' said Will.

Aish fetched the Hunter's spear, which she had propped against the wall, and gave it to Figgy for his staff of office. He stood up to accept it, and Utterly thought

263

he seemed to stand a little taller than before, and his eyes looked brighter, and his hair curlier, and she wondered if he had perhaps been altered more than any of them.

'And I shall be Assistant Watcher, if Figgy will accept me,' declared Miss Inshaw. 'For although it is lovely to be home safe, I confess I cannot imagine spending a whole night within four walls again, without being able to see the stars, or hear the night-time life of the trees going on around me. And I cannot conceive of returning to the dull things I used to fill my time with; embroidery, and reading novels, and suchlike. I had a great affection for Figgy when I thought he was a dog, which I cannot alter now that I know him to be a man. So I thought, if the Rafterys are removing here, then Figgy and I might make a little home for ourselves at Nutcombe Lodge. Several of its walls are standing still, and there are plenty of scattered beams and floorboards we could turn into a sort of shelter, for when the weather is inclement.'

'But Liz!' cried Mr Inshaw. 'What will people say when they hear you are living in a tree-house, with a common soldier?'

'Oh, calm yourself, dear Francis,' said Jane Raftery. 'They will say, "Miss Inshaw is very lucky", for Mr Figgis is a most *un*common soldier. Then they will say, "And *we* are very lucky too, for we live on the Autumn Isles, where people may do what pleases them, and not in stuffy old England, where they mayn't."'

After tea, they crossed the river and walked into the woods. They met some gentlemen there who had ridden over from Swaylebury, drawn by rumours of strange happenings. But already the magic was having its usual effect on people's memories, and, having wandered in wonderment among the trees a while, the gentlemen believed the wood had been there always. 'I had forgot how old your oaks are, Inshaw,' one said cheerfully. 'There's a fortune in timber here.'

'Ah,' said Mr Inshaw, 'but my sister and I will never cut them down.'

'Your sister, Inshaw? I thought she had been struck by lightning?'

'I am much recovered, sir,' said Miss Inshaw. 'But Francis, will we not need the money these trees would fetch? I recall you being most concerned about our finances before I went away.'

'I dare say something will turn up,' said Mr Inshaw. Having her and Jane back had restored his natural optimism.

Now that the trees were free from the Underwoods, they did not feel so wild any more, or at least felt wild only in good ways. By next summer they would be as homely as the Dizzard, Utterly thought. The people of Barrowchurch would let their pigs and cattle forage among them, and collect the fallen branches for their fires.

Mr Inshaw and his sister, with the Rafterys and Figgy

Dan, walked over to Nutcombe Lodge to see what might be salvaged. Aish said her leg was too sore for her to walk so far, but really she could walk well enough, with the aid of a stick. She just wanted to be alone with Will, and when the others had gone, the two of them went up together onto the Knoll.

There they found bits of the poor old church scattered all down the slopes, and the Barrowchurch Oak fallen in ruin. In the hole beneath the old tree's roots was the stone door, still standing upright, though somewhat askew.

'Are you sure the Hunter's door is closed?' Will asked.

Aish looked sideways at him. 'Can't you tell, Will Dark? You are Watcher on Wildsea, and have met all manner of magics. Surely you can tell by now when another world is brushing its skirts against our own?'

Will smelled the air, and listened as hard as he could with his eyes closed, and put his hand on one of the upright stones as if he were feeling for its heartbeat, but he could not detect any of the smells or sounds or feelings he associated with the Underwoods. And when he stooped and went through the door, it led him only into a narrow burial chamber, whose roof had split in places to let the daylight in.

There, when they had heaved a few fallen stones aside, they found the remains of old oak chests, and shining dimly in them golden brooches, collars, and a great gold shield. 'Well here is the answer to Cousin Francis's money troubles,' said Will, lifting treasures aside and finding more treasures beneath. 'Barrowchurch Knoll is a veritable goldmine!'

But Aish had made her own find, in the centre of the old chamber. The crumbling bones were so small Will thought at first it was the skeleton of a child she was stooping over, but Aish said the man they had belonged to had looked much taller when he was young and had some flesh on him. She knelt down and kissed the top of the little skull, and said, 'Here is my poor friend Lorn, whom I commanded to throw those things into the deep so long ago. And would not it have saved us all a peck of troubles if he had done as I told him to?'

Will looked at her as she sat there like Prince Hamlet with the skull in her hand. 'Aish,' he said, 'you are so very long-lived, and my span is only likely to be the usual three-score years and ten. I fear that in a blink of your eye you will be contemplating *my* dry old bones.'

Aish put down the grim *memento mori* and hugged him close. 'Time is what we make of it on Wildsea,' she said. 'And we shall have a whole lifetime together, Will Dark, I promise.'

'So my only other question,' said Will, 'is, how am I to take my dear wife home to Sundown Watch? For the way through the woods is closed, and she has an aversion to travelling by sea.'

'Oh, that is all dealt with,' said Aish. 'Egg has devised

a most ingenious system. All we shall need is Captain Varley's help, and around a hundred square foot of fresh-cut turf.'

❖

Utterly and Egg had slipped away together too. Egg had brought his knapsack with him, and he opened it proudly to show Utterly what lay inside.

'It is a cake,' she said. 'But it is a bit squashed.'

'Because I've lugged it all the way from Wildsea! It is one of Mrs Skraeveling's cakes.'

'But Egg, I am still too full from luncheon to enjoy it! How I regret my third helping of treacle pudding now!'

''Tis not a cake for *eating*, Utterly. I ain't brung it all this way to *eat*. If I had, I would've eaten it already. 'Tis a cake for giving away.'

Utterly gaped at him. 'Egg? Are you feeling quite yourself?'

'Come on, you goose,' said Egg, lacing up the knap-sack again. 'While there's still enough light to see by.'

The day was fading fast, and the shades of twilight lay beneath the trees along the river – the old, plain, ordinary trees that had stood there always. Only the dried-out waterweed that festooned the lower branches and draped itself around the palings of the footbridge showed where the flood had roared by.

Utterly stood watching while Egg went to the water's edge. 'I brought you something,' he said, speaking loudly to the river. 'Good as my word I am, see? It's one of Mrs Skraeveling's cakes. You won't taste better, not if you swim all the way to London town.'

There was no answer. 'I reckon she's just shy 'cos you're with me,' Egg told Utterly. He crouched down and put the cake in the water, giving it a gentle shove to send it out into mid-stream. It drifted a short way, turning circles on the current, and slowly sank.

Egg stood up and licked a few spare raisins off his hands. 'A "thank you, Egg" would've been nice,' he grumbled. 'Ain't got no manners, some people.' But secretly he was glad the river girl had not shown herself to Utterly. It felt good to have some magic that was his alone.

They turned and were about to walk back to the house when there was a swirl in the water behind them, as if a big fish had risen. When they looked round, the river was still empty, but something lay on the planks of the foot-bridge, so pale that it seemed to glow in the twilight. Egg went and picked it up, stood staring at it for a moment, then brought it to Utterly, shaking his head.

'It is my stone fish!' she said, taking it from him.

'The same one old Hyssop swiped?' said Egg. 'I wonder how the river girl got her hands on it?'

30

HOMEWARD

The sea was an altered character too. It seemed livelier. The wind that plumped the *Whimbrel*'s sails whipped it into choppy little waves. They glowed like bottle-glass when the sun shone through them, and kept crisping into white crests.

The *Whimbrel*'s foredeck had been covered with wetted tarpaulins, and on the tarpaulins a lawn of fresh-cut turfs had been spread out, so that Aish could sit there with the grass tickling up between her toes as if she were still in the fields of Summertide. 'So this is the sea,' she said, looking around as the *Whimbrel* left Summertide Town behind. 'It is much *bouncier* than I had expected.'

Back across the island-freckled sea they sailed, past Lamontane, Seapitts, Gorsedd, Holt, and Finnery.

Utterly looked at those places with fresh interest now. On the outward voyage she had thought them poor, dull sorts of islands, offering none of the mysteries Wildsea held. But now she knew there was magic even on sleepy Summertide, so who could tell what might be stirring in the mountains of Lamontane, or the deep-quarried slatey heart of Seapitts?

'We should visit all the islands,' said Egg. 'We could get Captain Varley to take us next summer. Or we could go through Aish's entrance to the Underwoods and walk – I bet we could find our way out on Lamontane, or even further off – why, we could walk to France, or India, or Timbuctoo . . .'

'You could not,' said Aish, firmly. 'The door on Wildsea will stay shut, for there are things far worse than the Hunter in the depths of that forest, and you do not want to go disturbing them.'

'Stick to sailing, young Egg,' agreed Captain Varley. 'There'll always be a berth for you aboard the *Whimbrel*.'

Utterly thought how grand it would be to spend a whole summer just sailing from one island to the next, and exploring each one in turn, and finding out which things were different there, and which the same. But then she remembered she would be elsewhere next summer. Her memories of the Underwoods and the Hunter were fading fast, as memories of magic always do (had he *really* had antlers? And could he *really* have been eaten by a whale?)

but her memory of the ancient ocean she had visited was clear and sharp in her mind's eye, and in her mind's ear she could still hear the Gorm saying, '*You must come to me, and dwell with me in the deeps,*' and her own self replying, '*When spring comes again, I will go into the sea and find you.*'

Which meant that this summer, which was already half worn-out, was the last summer she would know on Wildsea. And it would be followed by the last autumn, and the last winter, and the last spring, and when summer came again, she would be gone.

Was this how people felt when the doctors gave them just six months to live, Utterly wondered. It was like a constant, secret leave-taking. The *Whimbrel* put in at Merriport and she bade farewell to Captain Varley thinking, *I may never meet him again.* The mowers were at work in the steep golden fields behind the town, and she watched their scythes flash and breathed the scent of new-cut hay and thought, *I might not ever see another harvest.* On the way over the hill she saw that the foxgloves were all gone to seed, except for a few late ones which still held up a flower or two, and she thought, *I might never hear another bee go bumbling into a foxglove-bell.* She had felt a whisper of this feeling when she came home from the Hidden Lands, but now it felt real. She was coming to the very end of being a child. It was exciting, because all sorts of adventures lay ahead of her. But it was sad too, and she began to wish she had not promised the Gorm she would come in the spring, but had said the spring after next, or the spring of five years from now, or maybe ten.

They came across St Chyan's Common, and the grass was leaning sideways in a wind from the west, and Mr and Mrs Skraeveling and the Dearloves were waiting outside the gate of Sundown Watch to welcome them, and everything looked so exactly as it always had it made Utterly cry. But everyone was too happy and busy to notice, so she forced herself to smile, and after a little while, when they were all in the drawing room, and Uncle Will was telling of their adventures, and Mrs Dearlove was quizzing Aish about the fashions on Summertide, she found that her sadness had passed, or at least, it had folded itself away into a little attic part of her, where it could wait in secret until she needed it.

She left them to their talk and went upstairs, stopping to stroke the little wooden tortoise on the landing newel post, in case he had missed her. The upper part of the house smelled of fresh paint. In the Watcher's study a brand new window had been fitted to replace the one the Gorm had smashed, and the sea-light poured through it to fall upon the ranked volumes of the Watchers' Log and the collection of curiosities that the late Mr Andrewe Dark had gathered from the shore. Utterly carefully added her chalk stone to the collection, opening it so both halves could be seen; the half with the stone fish, and the matching half with its impression.

Then she went to the window. The wind was making the curtains sway. Out on the brim of the sea, as if they had never been away, the Hidden Lands were waiting.

Utterly stood and watched them. The big, tall-mountained island she had once visited lay far and blue in the afternoon sunlight, and she thought she could see others beyond it, farther still, faint purple and lilac outlines on the very edge of sight.

Down in the cove big, lazy waves were breaking, and as each wave drew back she heard it whisper, '*Utterly . . .*'

ACKNOWLEDGEMENTS

Thank you so much to everyone at DFB who has worked so hard to make and publicize this book, and to Paddy Donnelly for the lovely cover and illustrations. Thanks too to my agent, Philippa Milnes-Smith, for her encouragement and enthusiasm, to Sarah Reeve for all those inspirational walks in the wild woods, and to Sarah McIntyre, whose endless creative energy is also an inspiration. And thanks also to YOU, for reading Utterly's adventures, because there wouldn't be much point in writing them down if you didn't. Everyone on Wildsea says hi.

ABOUT THE AUTHOR

Philip Reeve is the author of many acclaimed and bestselling books, including *Railhead*, *Here Lies Arthur* and *Mortal Engines*, which was made into a major movie. He has also collaborated with Sarah McIntyre on several hugely popular, highly-illustrated stories including *Pugs of the Frozen North* and the *Roly-Poly Flying Pony* series. His books have won the Carnegie Medal, the Smarties Prize and many other awards. He lives with his wife and son on Dartmoor.

DISCOVER UTTERLY'S
FIRST MAGICAL ADVENTURE

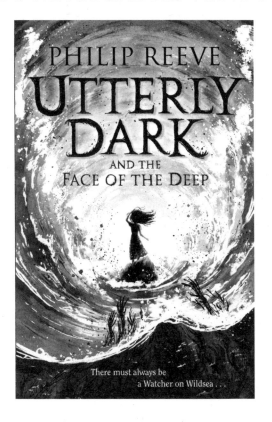

As the entrancing power of the sea fills Utterly Dark's dreams, so it will seep into your heart as you read this thrilling story about friendship, magic and the ocean. A novel full of mystery and delight, from bestselling, award-winning author Philip Reeve.

David Fickling Books